The Dark Hollows of West Virginia

Mack Samples

quarrier press

Charleston, West Virginia

Quarrier Press
Charleston, WV

Book and cover design: Mark S. Phillips

Library of Congress Control Number: 2010938280
ISBN 13: 978-1-891852-73-2
ISBN 10: 1-891852-73-6

10 9 8 7 6 5 4 3 2 1

Printed in the United States of America

Distributed by:

West Virginia Book Co.
1125 Central Avenue
Charleston, WV 25302

www.wvbookco.com

ACKNOWLEDGEMENTS

My sincere appreciation to long time friend, Dr. Ragina Copeland, for editing the manuscript of this novel. Ragina was a long time professor and administrator at WVU—Parkersburg. She is now retired and makes her home in Virginia.

And, as always, a big "Thank You" to my wife, Thelma, who always does a second edit and is very understanding when I retreat to my "man cave" in the basement to do my serious writing.

Finally, thanks to all of those West Virginians who have "led lives of quiet desperation" and inspired me to write this novel.

THE TRANSPARENT COUNTY, WEST VIRGINIA ECONOMIC DEVELOPMENT COMMITTEE

FRANK MCCRAY—Superintendent of Schools of Transparent County and antique car buff

REVEREND ALVIN "DEACON" BARGER—Transparent County's best known and most highly respected minister

CECIL BLYER—Owner and operator of a very successful sawmill and lumber yard

SIDNEY CURTIN—President of the Transparent Citizens Bank and Chairman of the Committee

HAROLD BLANEY—West Virginia University Extension Agent assigned to Transparent County

HANS JORGENSON—Transparent County's most successful young farmer

JOHN WESLEY FREMONT—Transparent County native in the process of building a regional home construction business

"NO HIT" STALNAKER—Legendary Transparent County athlete and a member of the Transparent County Commission

TRANSPARENT, WEST VIRGINIA
AUGUST 10, 2008

The Reverend Alvin "Deacon" Barger set his coffee cup on the sink about 9:00 a.m., Saturday morning, August 10, 2008, and grabbed his straw hat off the counter. "I'm going to ride over and talk with 'No Hit' for a little while," he said to his wife.

"What are you gonna' talk with him about?" his wife asked.

"Oh, the Economic Development Committee has been talking about some property that we might be interested in over in his area. He and I might take a look at it."

"Deacon," as he was known by just about everybody in the area, walked out into his garage. He picked up one of his daughter's baseball bats and laid it behind the seat of his pickup. It has to be a baseball bat, he thought to himself.

He fired up his truck and drove toward the town of Transparent, West Virginia. He had to go through town in order to get to the Stalnaker place.

Frank McCray, Superintendent of Schools in Transparent County, and a member of the Transparent County Economic Committee, walked into the Transparent Citizen's Bank on Saturday morning at about the same time that Deacon Barger left his kitchen. He was greeted with a warm smile from Jeanie Sprouse, one of the tellers.

"What can I do for you this morning, Mr. McCray?" she asked.

"Well, I have a somewhat unusual request," he replied.

"I want to cash in a couple of CDs, the ones that are in my name only, and I want the money in cash. I will take it in the largest denominations that you have. Do they still print one-thousand-dollar bills?"

"No, I'm afraid hundreds is the best I can do. That's the largest bill in circulation right now. I guess at one time there were thousand-dollar bills around, but I've never seen one."

"Neither have I," said Frank. "In fact, it wasn't too long ago that a hundred-dollar bill was pretty rare."

Jeanie pulled up his account information on the computer and saw that Frank and his wife, Gina, had a total of five CDs. Three of them were held jointly. The two that were in his name only were the result of money he had stashed away from antique car deals that he was always negotiating. The CD's came to a total of $33,704.

"Are you sure you want this in cash?" Jeanie Sprouse asked with a slight squint in one eye.

"Yes, I definitely want it in cash," he replied.

"Well, I guess I had better run this by Mr. Curtin," she said. "I have never distributed this much cold cash before."

"Fine," said Frank.

Jeanie walked into Sidney Curtin's office. Mr. Curtin came back out with her. He walked over to Frank and extended his hand.

"What you doin,' Frank, skipping the country?

Frank smiled and replied, "No, actually Sidney, Wes Fremont told me about a man down around Tampa, who has a nice old '55 Cadillac that he might sell. I've been talking with the guy on the phone. He says he wants thirty-five thousand for it, but I'm going to fly down there this weekend and wave some cash at him. I might be able to get it for a little less. School starts soon, you know, and I won't be able to get away. I just might drive that Caddy home in a couple of days."

"Sounds like a good plan to me," said Sidney. He walked back behind the counter and coached Jeanie about how to handle the transaction.

Frank left the bank with the cash in a small briefcase. He shoved the money under the seat of his Ford F150 and drove out of town. But he was not headed for Florida. He was going down the road a few miles and pay a visit to Deacon Barger. But when he got within about two miles of his house, he recognized Deacon's big Ford F350 diesel truck coming toward him. Frank let him pass, went on down the road about five hundred yards, and turned around. He thought to himself that this might even work out better. He decided he would stay a respectable distance behind Deacon and see where the old boy was headed. By the time they got to the town of Transparent, two cars had worked their way in between them. Frank kept an eye on the big, noisy diesel truck and followed it through town.

Just as Deacon had told his wife, he was headed out to a dark hollow on the other side of town to pay a call on "No Hit" Stalnaker, President of the Transparent County Commission and member of the Transparent County Economic Development Committee. But as he drove past the local Go-Mart convenience store, he spotted No Hit gassing up his Toyota Corolla.

It was mid-morning but the August sun was already brutal. No Hit was wearing a short-sleeved white shirt unbuttoned in front. Deacon pulled his truck into one of the parking places out to the side of the store, retrieved the baseball bat out from behind his seat, and made a circuitous walk towards No Hit so that he would not see him. Frank McCray had pulled in a couple of spaces down from Deacon's truck. He got out and stood beside the front fender of his F150, watching the preacher.

Deacon came up behind No Hit and without warning came down across the back of his neck with the baseball bat. No Hit went down on his knees not knowing what hit him. Deacon struck him again, this time with a home run swing across the back of the head. No Hit slumped to the ground, the gasoline nozzle still in his hand. Gasoline spilled out across his bare chest. Deacon started to hurry to his truck, but when he turned around, he found himself looking down the muzzle of a .380 automatic held by Frank McCray. Frank did not say hello or goodbye. He just pumped the seven rounds that were in the clip into the chest of the Reverend Alvin Deacon Barger. Barger fell back against No Hit's Toyota and slid to the ground. Only a few feet separated Barger from No Hit. Frank McCray raced to his truck and sped out of the parking lot.

There were three other vehicles at the gas pumps when the altercation started, two pickup trucks and an older model Chevy Blazer. The man driving one of the pickups was in by the cash register. The man in the other pickup was starting to pull away from the pumps. The woman driving the Blazer was still filling her tank when she heard the shots. When she turned around, she had a very good view of Frank McCray as he hurried toward his truck. The driver of the pickup, who was inside, rushed out to where No Hit was lying and knelt down to see if he was alive. The young girl who was working the register also came running out. "He's alive," the kneeling man yelled. "I can feel a pulse." He moved over a few feet to look at Deacon Barger. "This one's dead, no doubt about it."

The man who was pulling away from the pumps slammed on his brakes and jumped out of his truck. He grabbed his cell phone and dialed 911. "There's been a shooting at the Go-

Mart," the man yelled into the phone, unaware of the battering of No Hit Stalnaker. "I think it was Frank McCray who did the shooting. He flew out of the parking lot in a Ford F150 and headed down the road toward his house."

The 911 dispatcher immediately put the report onto the scanner. The on-duty deputy was on the other end of the county, but he sped toward the Go-Mart. The dispatcher also tried to call the sheriff. He called both his home and cell phone but got no answer on either of them. He also tried the State Police detachment, but got no answer there either.

Frank McCray drove toward Charleston, avoiding the main highways. He picked his way through the countryside on one-lane roads and even took one short cut on an unpaved road. He just cruised along so as not to attract any attention. Many thoughts were racing through his mind as he finally steered the F150 up the hill to the Charleston Airport. But he kept wondering what was going on between Reverend Barger and No Hit. He had no idea why Deacon would brutally attack the legendary baseball player. But it sure provided him with an opportunity that he had not anticipated. He had originally planned to ask Deacon to ride over to the church with him to look over a remodeling project they were considering for the annex. As it turned out, that plan did not have to be carried out.

Frank knew he was going to have to move quickly, much more quickly than he had originally planned. He was very aware that at least two or three people had witnessed the beating and shooting. They had seen him get into his truck. There was no doubt in his mind that there would soon be an APB out on him and the F150. But he kept to his game plan. He drove the Ford into the long term parking garage at the airport, walked over to the terminal and rented a car. It was a Ford Focus. He, of course, paid cash.

As he drove back down the airport hill, he knew that he was going to have to be very careful with his route. He decided to drive up I-79 to Clarksburg and take Route 50 East all the way to Washington, D.C. From there, he had initially planned to take I-95 up the east coast to New York City. But when he reached the eastern panhandle of West Virginia, he decided to avoid the Washington D.C./Baltimore/Philadelphia megalopolis and picked up I-81 north to where it intersected with I-80 in Pennsylvania. He followed I-80 into the Big Apple.

He was betting that the authorities would find his truck at the Charleston airport before too long and would be scanning all of the airline rosters. As it turned out, they did not find his truck until around noon on Monday. Frank arrived in New York City on Sunday, August 11. He had parked the rental car in a hotel parking lot and caught a taxi over to the train station.

Frank had studied the Amtrak schedule carefully and had his escape route to the West planned well. He spent the afternoon and night in Penn Station. On Monday, he boarded the Amtrak Lake Shore Limited and was on his way to Chicago. So far he had not even gotten a suspicious look from anyone. Once he got to the Grand Central Station in Chicago, he booked passage on the Amtrak Empire Builder to Seattle, Washington. He was traveling by coach. He had been using his own name when he purchased the tickets and was surprised that no one asked for any identification. All of his transactions were made in cash. In accordance with his game plan, he got off the Empire Builder in Havre, Montana.

He poked around the used car lots in Havre for a couple of hours and spotted a 98 Chevy pickup with four-wheel drive. Frank was a car man. One of his passions in life was antique cars. He knew what to look for when checking out a used vehicle. The Chevy was in excellent shape. It had a nearly new set of all-weather tires on it. He was able to buy it for ten thousand dollars, cash money. He took his first big risk at this point, using his own name in the transaction and showing his driver's license. He informed the car dealer that he was moving to Skagway, Alaska.

"As soon as I get settled there, I'll send you my Post Office Box number so you will know where to send the title and permanent plates."

The dealer put Montana temporary tags on the pickup. Frank headed north into Canada. He figured he had not taken a huge risk, but it was a risk. Yet he doubted that the police network would be checking out car sales in Montana. At any rate there would be no paper trail of his transactions.

Frank was very apprehensive as he approached the Canadian border. It was quite possible that the Canadian authorities had been alerted. There might very well be a picture of him posted on the wall right beside the border guard. In a world where the instant transfer of information was commonplace, it was even more than possible. It was probable. He had a passport that was issued in 2004 when he and his wife, Gina, had spent a couple of weeks in Europe. The passport showed that it was issued in West Virginia. He had a West Virginia driver's license. The Chevy was wearing a temporary license plate from Montana.

He parked the truck and walked up to the desk. He was greeted with a smile and a nod. Frank showed his passport and asked if he needed further identification. The border guard looked over the passport and handed it back to him,

"You going into Canada on business, or are you sight seeing?"

"Actually, I'm just passing through," said Frank. "I am

exploring a job up in Alaska and decided I would just drive the Alaskan Highway and look the country over while I was at it. I rode the train out to Havre and bought the truck." Frank nodded toward the truck as he spoke.

"Well I hope you have a pleasant trip," said the border guard. "You picked a good time of the year to make the drive."

"Thanks a lot," said Frank as he turned to go to the Silverado.

"You betcha," said the guard.

Frank had been intrigued by Skagway, Alaska, ever since he read Jack London's *Call of the Wild* in high school. Before he had made his big move, he spent some time on the internet reading about historic and modern Skagway. It appeared to him to be a very good place to hide.

After spending several days in Calgary, Canada, where he purchased some clothes and enjoyed some good meals, he headed northwest and picked up the Alaskan Highway. He took his time and thoroughly enjoyed the drive. It was something he had always wanted to do. He had always heard there were some long, desolate segments on the highway; he soon found them. But he didn't mind at all. Right before he got to Whitehorse, Canada, he took the Klondike Highway southwest into the Alaskan panhandle and rolled into Skagway on August 28th.

Skagway was a summer tourist town, and the season was not quite over when Frank McCray arrived. The little town was booming and motel rooms were sky high. The cheapest one he could find was $150 per day. He still had a little better than twenty thousand dollars in his little brief case, so he was not yet concerned. He had learned from his internet reading that the town would shrink to about 850 people when the tourists left. Then the rent would drop drastically.

IN THE TRANSPARENT COUNTY SHERIFF'S OFFICE AUGUST 12, 2008

On Monday morning, August 12th, two days after the terrible scene at the local Go-Mart, a tearful Gina McCray was sitting in the Transparent County sheriff's office. Sheriff Clayton McKee and two of his deputies were asking her questions.

"Did Frank leave you a note, or give you any indication that he was leaving?"

"No," Gina answered without further comment.

"Do you have any idea why Frank might want to shoot Deacon?"

"No, I don't have a clue. As you probably know, Frank and I have attended his church for several years. They always appeared to have a cordial relationship. And, as you also know, all three of the men involved in the incident were on the county economic development committee. I know that committee often had heated debates but I can't imagine that anything happened there that would motivate Frank to want to shoot anyone. In fact, I just cannot imagine Frank shooting anyone. He was a quiet, gentle man. I'm just baffled by the entire affair."

"And you don't have any idea where he might have gone?"

"Absolutely not," Gina replied. "He told me last week that he was going down to Florida to look at a Cadillac. I thought nothing of that because he goes and looks at cars all the time."

"Did you know that he cashed in two substantial CDs at the bank on Saturday morning?"

"No, I didn't know that," Gina answered truthfully.

"Have you and Frank been having domestic problems lately?"

"Not at all," said Gina. "I thought everything was just fine."

"You know that No Hit died this morning at Charleston Area Medical Center," the sheriff continued. "So what we are dealing with here is a double homicide. At this point we don't have a motive for either of them. All three of these gentlemen were well respected in our community."

"No, I didn't know No Hit had died," Gina replied. "Do you know why Deacon was beating him over the head? Maybe that had something to do with Frank's actions."

"Well, at first blush, you would think that it was all tied together some way or another. But right now we have no evidence of that."

"I just cannot imagine why Deacon would want to harm No Hit, Gina said, as she began to sob again. "Just look at what he has done for the kids in the county." Then she began to cry almost hysterically.

Sheriff McKee looked at her for a minute. "Why don't you go home and get some rest, Gina? We may want to talk with you later."

Gina McCray returned to the dark, lonely hollow where she lived. She was now alone in the world. She had no children. She was for all practical purposes a thirty-six year old widow because regardless of whether or not they ever caught up with Frank, he was gone from her life. She was, however, comforted by the fact that she was financially well off.

After Gina left his office, Sheriff McKee looked at his deputies. "You guys see anything that I didn't see. She looked pretty clueless to me."

Both deputies concurred.

As badly as he hated to interrogate grieving widows, the sheriff decided he would drive out and talk with Reverend Barger's wife. He thought perhaps she might hold the key to the entire situation, and he wanted to get this mess behind him as soon as possible. When he got to the Barger homestead, he spotted her sitting alone on the porch with her head down. He had never met her personally but he had seen her around with Deacon. He approached the porch.

"Mrs. Barger," he began, "I'm Sheriff McKee. I'd like to ask you a few questions."

"Come on up and sit down," she replied. "Get out of that hot sun."

"Thanks," said the sheriff. He plopped down on the glider and pulled at his collar. "It has been a hot spell, hasn't it? First off, I am really sorry about your husband. I know he was a well-respected man in our community. Everyone is in shock. I guess I'm not very good at condolences, but I really am sorry. I hesitated bothering you at his point but I thought you might be able to help me get a head start on this situation. Do you have any idea at all why your husband would want to attack No Hit Stalnaker?"

"No, I really don't," she responded. "You know my daughter played baseball on his team. I know they talked some when Deacon took her to practice. Oftentimes No Hit would bring her home after practice and they would chat some here in the yard. They were not close friends but always appeared to be cordial to one another. No Hit and his family attended our church, but not on a regular basis. Of course you know they were both on the Economic Development Committee. But I never once heard my husband say an unkind word about Mr. Stalnaker. I am as puzzled about this as anyone. I just never thought my husband was capable of killing anyone."

"Well, Mrs. Barger, I believe that anyone is capable of anything if they have the right motivation. There must have been something that set your husband off. We need to find out what that something was. You know, we read in the papers all the time that men who go on shooting sprees are usually just normal people. Something just sets them off, I guess."

"I just can't imagine," she replied softly.

"I don't know your oldest daughter," Mrs. Barger. "How old is she?"

"She is a very mature eleven, and as you may have heard, a very talented athlete."

"No, I hadn't heard that," said the sheriff. "Did the Reverend say anything to you before he left the house on Saturday, say where he was going or anything like that?"

"Yes, he did," she said. "He said very matter-of-factly that he was going to drive over and talk with No Hit about some property. I just figured it had something to do with that committee they are on."

"Is your daughter home, Mrs. Barger?"

"No, both of the children are with my sister. She is supposed to bring them home today."

"I really hate to bring this up, Mrs. Barger, but what about the other side of the equation? Do you have any idea why Frank McCray got involved in this situation?"

"Now that's the thing that has me totally baffled," she replied. "The McCrays went to our church. I always thought Frank and Deacon were pretty good friends. Frank's wife, Gina, served as the church secretary and treasurer. I am sorry to say I have no answer for that question."

Sheriff McKee decided to leave it there. Mrs. Barger appeared to be holding up very well, but he did not want to push the envelope too much. The one thing she had said that caught his attention was that their daughter played on No Hit's baseball team. Perhaps, he thought, something transpired in one of the games that had pissed the Reverend off. He knew how upset parents got over sporting events. It was possible that Deacon was upset about something and just wanted to rough No Hit up a little, then got carried away in the process. But Frank McCray did not fit into that theory at all. Sheriff McKee had one more grieving widow to talk with, but this was certainly not the day to do that. No Hit had been dead only a few hours.

Sheriff McKee walked into his office on the morning of Tuesday the 13th, and sat down at his desk. He was seventy-one years old and had less than five months left to serve, but no one ever thought of him as an old man. Most of his hair was still with him, albeit a bit grey. His broad shoulders weren't stooped a bit, and every morning as soon as his feet hit the floor, he cracked fifty pushups. While he was still a fine physical specimen, he had developed a fairly serious hearing problem. He had to really concentrate when he was talking with people, especially women. His twenty-eight years in the United States Navy, much of that time on the deck of an aircraft carrier, had done major damage to his ears.

But Clayton McKee had no regrets about his time in the service. For the most part he had enjoyed the Navy. Best of all, it had provided him with a comfortable retirement. He had retired as a Master Chief (E-8). He had spent about ten years working in the Seattle, Washington area before he returned to his native West Virginia, in 1998. He had planned to just take it easy. But after about a year he became a little restless. So he decided to throw his hat in the ring for sheriff when the 2000 election came around.

Eight people filed for the slot on the Democratic ticket, and Clayton won a narrow victory. The Republicans offered only token resistance, so he won the general election easily. To his surprise, he really enjoyed being sheriff and had a very successful first term. He filed for re-election in 2004 and won the Democratic primary by a landslide.

Even though he was now trying hard not to, he was losing interest in the job. Just recently he had decided that he would just go through the motions and ride out the last few months of his term. There was no doubt he was going to have to deal with meth labs and illegal selling of pain pills, but he never expected to get caught up in anything as intriguing as the series of events that had transpired on Saturday.

He arrived at the office a little earlier than usual. The eerie silence of the place made him relax a bit. He shuffled a few papers on his desk and decided it was time he got his priorities straight. As far as crime was concerned, Frank McCray had taken care of half the problem. He really did not have to figure out why Deacon Barger had beaten No Hit to death. Frank McCray had closed that case. Deacon was dead and that was that. So he figured he had better devote his efforts toward finding Frank.

The first thing he needed to do was to file a report to the National Crime Information Center (NCIC), so the entire nation would be looking for him. He was glad he had waited a couple of days because now, in addition to Frank's picture, he could add a possible location. Even though he was not really sure which way Frank went when he left town, he had called the State Police and the Charleston Police Department about two hours after the incident and told them to be on the lookout for the Ford F150. Some of the bystanders reported that Frank headed toward Charleston, but Sheriff McKee figured he could have easily altered that route. By the time word got around, Frank had already parked the pickup in the Charleston Airport parking garage.

About noon on Monday, August 12, the West Virginia State Police sent a trooper to check the parking lots at the train station and airport. About 2:00 p.m., he discovered Frank's pickup in the airport parking garage. After spending a couple of hours going over the rosters of the flights that had left Charleston on Saturday, Sunday and Monday, the trooper concluded that Frank McCray did not take a flight out of Charleston, at least not under his real name. On an impulse he walked over to the Hertz Rental area and discovered that Frank had rented a Ford Focus and told the Hertz people that he would turn it in down in Tampa, Florida, in a few days.

So along with the description of Frank and a picture, Sheriff McKee informed the NCIC that Frank was believed to be headed toward Florida in a Hertz Ford Focus. By the time the report was received by NCIC, Frank McCray was rolling along the banks of Lake Erie on the Amtrak Lake Front Limited.

There was not much else the sheriff could do. He would tell all of his deputies to keep an eye out for Frank, but, somehow, he doubted if Frank was in the area or would come back any time soon. So Sheriff McKee decided that he would try to figure out why Frank shot Deacon Barger. He would wait until after Deacon's funeral before he talked with his widow again. But he thought he might start with the remaining members of the Transparent County Economic Development Committee. A good place to begin, he figured, was with Sidney Alvin Curtin.

SIDNEY CURTIN AND THE ECONOMIC DEVELOPMENT COMMITTEE

Transparent County had some beautiful country. Like nearly every West Virginia county, it had a river valley and a multitude of smaller tributaries that found their way to the main river. The primary road followed the river.

The homes that were scattered along the river were modest but presentable. The residents of the valley probably spent more money maintaining their lawns and surrounding environs than just about anybody else on the planet. The grass grew greener and the weeds grew faster than in most areas of the country. There was no need for fertilizer on the lawns. In the areas that could not be reached by a lawn mower, the unwanted weeds and brush became unsightly in no time at all. But those who lived in the lush valley made sure that nuisance growth was kept under control. They referred to the non-cultivated wild growth as "filth." It was an unwritten law in the valley that you had to keep your "filth" cut. Just about every household had a small fortune tied up in riding lawn mowers, push lawn mowers, weed eaters, and chain saws.

There were many secondary roads that turned off the main artery that followed the river. A turn up any of these roads usually led to beautiful farms that situated themselves along the banks of the tributaries. Neat farm houses, surrounded by well-kept barns and tool sheds, were a common sight. Most of the farms were supported by men and women who worked in the nearby towns in order to maintain the farms. The farms were a labor of love for these folks. They usually kept a few head of livestock and maintained a huge vegetable garden. The farms provided the residents with just about everything they ate, but they had to work elsewhere to enjoy the perks of modern life such as SUVs, satellite television, washers, dryers, and summer trips to Myrtle Beach.

Their children were their pride and joy. They clothed them in the best possible manner, drove them around to all the school and community functions, and tried to instill a work ethic into them by requiring them to do some farm chores. 4-H and FFA were the order of the day for these kids. Sidney Alvin Curtin was the proud owner of one of these beautiful homesteads.

Sidney was an average-sized man with a slight build who could trace his family back for five generations in West Virginia. His steely blue eyes complemented his rather dark skin. His 170 pounds were well distributed over his five-foot-ten-inch frame. There was a commanding presence about him. Any time he was a member of a group there was never any doubt about who was in charge.

Sidney was every ounce a local boy. He grew up on the family farm just outside of town, graduated from Transparent High School, and worked his way through Fairmont State College. His outstanding scholarship at Fairmont State, along with a special relationship that he had developed with the president, got him admitted to the Wharton School of Business with a full assistantship. As soon as he acquired the cherished MBA, he headed back to the hills and got himself a job at the Transparent Citizen's Bank. The bank management started him as a teller, but in no time at all, they had named him Vice President in charge of loans.

His parents had given up the farm where Sidney had grown up and moved into a retirement home just south of Charlotte,

North Carolina. Sidney and his siblings were all too busy getting educated and making a living to keep the place up. The house had nearly rotted down. The once-clean-as-a-whistle pasture fields and meadows now supported poplar trees a foot through. The place was located up one of the dark hollows just off the main road.

Once he got himself established at the bank, he bargained with his dad and his brothers and managed to get a deed to the old farm with only his name on it. He began devoting every minute of his spare time towards restoring the old home place to its original splendor. He razed the old house and soon had a crew on site clearing off the meadows and pasture fields. The only salvageable building on the old farm was the barn. He and his brothers had roofed it shortly before he had gone away to college and it was in excellent shape.

He decided that the barn would be a symbol of his ties with the past. Sidney soon had a paint crew working on it. After a coat of fresh red paint brought it back to life, he hired a professional sign maker paint SIDNEY ALVIN CURTIN FARM on both ends in big white letters. He then moved a small mobile home onto the property to live. Once he got the fences back in order, he borrowed enough money from his bank to purchase ten head of Black Angus cows. Sidney figured that the cows would not only help keep the pastures clean, but they would also produce some calves that would bring a nice price in the fall.

He continued to move up at the bank. In the winter of 2001, the president of the bank abruptly resigned and took a job in North Carolina. The Bank's Board of Directors, without much debate, moved Sidney into the job.

It wasn't long until Sidney's success at the bank and his activity on the old farm attracted the attention of a local young lady. One year after he had established himself on the farm, he married Mary Beth Hadley, the daughter of Transparent County's prosecuting attorney. No matter what else you could say about Mary Beth Hadley, no one denied that she was a looker.

Two years later, Sidney and Mary Beth constructed a large two-story house on the site where the original farmhouse was located. The brick mansion had four bedrooms, two baths and a huge triple garage. It was more house than they needed because the couple was childless after three years of marriage.

During the fall of 2005, Sidney decided that it was time to "give back" to the county that had been so good to him, so he put together The Transparent County Economic Development Committee and assumed the chairmanship.

The Committee met for the first time on January 7, 2006. Sydney was excited as the group got together for their first meeting. Here was a group of people who had gotten things done, action people. He could almost smell the smoke from the factories that these folks would bring to the county. He could almost see the lights bursting forth on the front of new restaurants and car dealerships. He did not even dare imagine all of the new money that would be flowing into his bank.

No introductions were necessary. Even though the membership did not often cross paths, they all knew each other. Some of them attended the same church. They all commonly bumped into each other at one of the local restaurants. The activities of their children also brought some of them together.

THE MEMBERSHIP

The secondary roads, which jutted off the main river valley road, were usually paved for just a mile or two, up to about where the small streams headed up. Then the roads usually turned to dirt and went straight up one of the hills and down into a dark hollow. Many times, a nice neat country residence could be found, even down in these dark hollows. Cecil Blyer occupied one of those dark hollows.

Now in his thirties, one look at him told you that he was a man who had worked hard for a living. His upper torso was solid muscle. His bull neck and shoulders indicated he had done some heavy lifting in his time. His rough hands left little doubt that he had not done his lifting in a weight room. He was a little unkempt at times, letting his ungroomed, light brown hair grow down to his shoulders. He always dressed in work clothes.

During his youth he was a self-trained skilled timber cutter. When employed, he made good money. There had been times, of course, when there was no timber work available. During those times Cecil had just grabbed any kind of work he could get. But he always managed to make a living. He was never on welfare.

During one of his prolonged timber jobs, he accumulated enough money to purchase about thirty acres of land. Other than a small level area right on the creek bank, the property consisted of rough hillside land. It was steep hillside, covered with small growth poplar trees and multi-flora rose bushes.

Cecil purchased a second-hand mobile home, pulled it into the hollow himself and began the laborious task of getting it ready for occupancy. He borrowed some equipment from one of the logging firms for which he had worked, and managed to get the mobile home up on blocks and level. There were few men indeed who could have managed to settle the trailer into position the way Cecil did.

There was a strong spring, which oozed out of the hill near the top of the property. Cecil harnessed the spring, ran it into a one-thousand-gallon plastic tank that he buried in the ground, and then piped the water on down to the trailer. He then had an endless supply of free, gravity-fed water. It was perfect spring water, the kind you paid a big price for in plastic bottles at the super market. There was electricity in the hollow, so he was able to connect to the power grid. But he only used the electricity for lights, a refrigerator, and a hot water tank. He installed a wood-burning stove for heat. Without consulting with any of the sanitation authorities, he ran his sewage into the creek.

Cecil lived alone in the mobile home for a time. He had few friends, none of whom ever stopped by. He had no interest in television. Most of his spare time was spent sitting by his stove in the winter, drinking whiskey and staring into the fire. Summers found him out on his makeshift porch, drinking beer and staring at the hillside across the creek from his residence. Cecil owned seven guns, and he loved to shoot them. He was not a collector of firearms. He was a user of firearms. He loved to hunt and paid no attention to the seasons. He hunted what he wanted to when he wanted to. But he always ate what he killed. Cecil was proud of the fact that he could kill a deer, field dress it, skin it out, cut it up, and cook it. He thought of himself as a mountain man.

Through hard work and sheer determination, Cecil soon had his own sawmill and lumberyard and was making more money than he had ever imagined. As his money supply increased, Cecil became much better known in the county. His success had caught the attention of Sidney Curtin. Sidney invited him to be a member of the Committee.

There was only one house up the hollow where Frank McCray lived. His house was located at the foot of the hill where the pavement ended. A stone-based road went on over the hill and connected with another road. But the road by his house was sparsely traveled.

Frank owned all the land on both sides of the quarter of a mile of paved road that led up to his house. He had built a sprawling ranch house on the most level part of the property with an unattached four-stall garage. Frank loved old cars and kept a '49 Mercury and a '51 Cadillac in the garage along with his Ford F150 pickup and the Cadillac SRX that his wife drove. He had owned, traded or sold several other old cars, but he could never bring himself to part with the '49 Merc or the '51 Caddy.

He was forty-two years old and had not taken very good care of his body. He had taken on a little too much middle, and his shoulders were showing just a slight slump. But he was one of the best-dressed men in the county. The superintendent's job, he figured, was a suit-and-tie job. Even when he was not officially working, he never went into town without putting on a nice shirt and usually a tie. Frank was self-conscious about having to wear glasses, so he always kept a pair of reading glasses in his shirt pocket. They were forever falling out when he bent over. Every time that happened Frank usually uttered a pretty string of profanity. He had a heavy head of dark hair that he kept short, making no attempt to comb it back.

He had come to the county in 1994 to accept a teaching

job. It was at Transparent High School that he later met and married his wife, Gina, a high school English teacher who had migrated in from Virginia. Gina was five years younger than Frank and had turned every male head in town when she arrived. She was one of those fortunate females who never had to worry about gaining weight. Her dark hair was her crowning glory. It was shoulder-length and always looked the same. During the early days of their marriage, the McCrays were a striking couple.

When Frank and Gina first got married they lived in a mobile home for a couple of years which they rented from a local farmer. The mobile home was located under a big white-oak tree on the farmer's property. It had been occupied by the farmer's daughter before she moved to Plano, Texas, to accept a nursing position. Frank, who had grown up in a medium-sized Pennsylvania town, loved the privacy that the location afforded and dreamed of buying the farm one day.

He began taking evening and summer classes at Marshall University. He soon earned a Master's Degree in Education. Gina got her real estate license, hooked up with a realtor in Charleston, and began selling real estate evenings and weekends. She saved every nickel she made at the moonlighting job. They were both members of the Transparent First Baptist Church. Even though she did not have time for it, Gina volunteered as secretary/treasurer for the church.

One year after acquiring his Master's degree, Frank was offered the principal's job at Transparent Middle School. He liked the administrative work and immediately began working on his Superintendent's Certificate at the Graduate College at Institute, West Virginia.

At the end of his fifth year as principal, he and Gina pooled their resources and bought the 147-acre tract at the end of the paved road where they had been renting the mobile home. It was a very secluded place and became black as coal when night arrived. Frank never liked outside lights. Some people called the dusk-to-dawn lights "security lights," but Frank always figured that those lights were an invitation for burglars. His theory was that if you kept it dark around your place, thieves and intruders wouldn't know anyone lived there. But he did have an array of floodlights that he could turn on with a switch in his bedroom.

He and Gina continued to live in the mobile while they built their house. Even though they were bringing home a lot of money each month, the couple struggled mightily for a time to make the mortgage payments, the payments on the two cars that they drove, and to pay back the money Frank had borrowed to acquire his graduate education. Then, out of the blue, Gina came into a sizable inheritance. They paid off all their debts. Gina gave up her teaching job. But she continued to sell real estate in the Charleston area.

Frank McCray was appointed Superintendent of Schools during the summer of 2004. His new-found prosperity allowed him to expand his passion, the purchase and restoration of old cars. He always drove one of them in any parade that occurred in the county. During the fall of 2007 the homecoming queen entered the football field on the fender of Frank's '51 Cadillac. His position with the school system and his stature in the community made him a natural choice to serve on the Transparent County Economic Development Committee.

Harold E. Blaney was forty-five years old when he arrived in town in 2004. He had taught agriculture in the public schools for a time before taking a job as a West Virginia University Extension Agent. He enjoyed his work as an Extension Agent and served in several counties. But in his forty-third year on the planet, his life took an unexpected left turn. His wife of twenty-one years went to a conference at Pipestem State Park down in southern West Virginia and fell head over heels in love with an itinerant musician. She left Harold two months later. The abruptness of her departure put Harold through a difficult time. He asked his superiors in Morgantown if could transfer to another county. The agent's position was vacant in Transparent County. Harold was offered the position and accepted it.

His arrival in Transparent County was met with mixed reactions. Rumors of his domestic troubles had preceded him. Some parents worried that he would not be a good role model for the 4-Hers with whom he would be working, even though some of those same parents had been married two or three times themselves. But others thought his experience would serve him well. Some of the area farmers were especially pleased that they were getting an agent with some agricultural experience.

He was a nice looking man and had the body of a twenty-five year old. All of his light brown hair was still with him. He had lifted weights since his college days. When Harold looked you in the eye, you felt it. He just had a way of grabbing you when he spoke.

After one year on the job and two years after his painful divorce, Harold put together enough money to purchase an out of the way abandoned small farm. He and his ex-wife had sold the home where they had enjoyed conjugal bliss for twenty years and had divided the money equally. The old farmhouse that he purchased was in bad shape, mostly due to neglect. He got it for a song. But Harold put his considerable skills to work and soon had the place livable. He thoroughly enjoyed the isolation that the dark holler afforded. He had never really lived in a place where there were no visible neighbors. What he really liked was that the house was so situated on the forty acres that no one would ever be able to build within sight of him. Yet all of the modern utilities were available. The really big plus was that he had his own gas well and could use all the free natural gas that he wanted.

Sidney Curtin soon became keenly aware of Harold's ability and invited him to serve on the Economic Development Committee. He accepted with pride.

Six-foot-four-inch Hans Jorgenson did not set many hearts aflutter when he walked down the street in Transparent. He was long and lean with a head that looked almost too big for him. Even though his body was not a thing of beauty, he was strong as a horse. He always wore a baseball cap so no one really knew for sure what his head looked like. He wore Carhartt coveralls during the winter. It did not matter where he went; he stayed with the Carhartts. During the hot summer months he wore khaki pants and always a long-sleeved white shirt. He had learned from his dad that a white long-sleeved cotton shirt provided protection from the sun and was relatively cool. The white shirts often became smudged with grease from his tractor so he changed every day.

He had lived in Transparent County all of his life. In fact, his travel outside the county had been very limited. After he finished high school in 1984, he just stayed on the family farm with his parents and three younger sisters. His parents were prosperous farmers. The main thrust of the farm was Black Angus cattle.

His dad had spent his life accumulating property. He owned a total of 740 acres of Transparent County real estate;

just about all of it farm land. It was all paid for. He had around two hundred head of cattle scattered around at the various locations that he had acquired. Hans shouldered much of the farm responsibility after high school.

His three sisters, Arlene, Maxine, and Eileen, had also stayed on the farm after high school. Arlene, the oldest, was an excellent farm hand and could handle a tractor as well as any man. She was just one year younger than Hans. Maxine was uncommonly strong for a woman and handled much of the heavy work around the barns. She could shoulder a sack of dairy feed with ease. Eileen tended to be a bit more domestic. She and her mother raised a big garden and canned or froze everything that the garden produced. Nothing went to waste. The Jorgensons were one of the few remaining families in the county who still kept a milk cow, chickens, and hogs. Except for the mechanized machinery, their lifestyle was not very different from those who had lived in the rural areas a hundred years before them.

The Jorgenson house was located about two miles off the main road. It was the only house on the gravel road that led to it. There was a rough road that went on over the hill. It was a four-wheel-drive access road, but there were a couple of hardy souls who lived on the other side of the hill. Huge maple and box elder trees shrouded the Jorgenson house from view until you were nearly on top of it. It was a big old farmhouse with six bedrooms. At one time, it had only one bath. But when the girls were in high school two more bathrooms had been added along with an ultra-modern kitchen. The Jorgenson spread was actually very comfortable.

Tragedy struck the Jorgenson family on January 7, 1998. Mr. and Mrs. Jorgenson had gone to town on a snowy morning to take care of some banking and to talk with a tax consultant at H & R Block. On the way home, a loaded log truck had skidded out of control and had hit the Jorgenson pickup head on. Both of them were killed instantly.

Hans, now twenty-eight years old, and single, decided that he had to keep the farm operation going. It had been, after all, his life. The three girls, none of whom was married, also decided to stay on. Although Hans was unaware of it until their death, his parents had maintained a one hundred thousand dollar life insurance policy on themselves.

The Jorgensons were not social. They had not participated in Farm Bureau, 4-H, nor any of the other farm-oriented organizations. All they had really ever known was work.

They were not religious people. The girls had attended a nearby church when they were very young, but had given it up when they were early teenagers. Hans had actually never been inside a church.

Despite his anti-social ways, Sydney Curtin thought Hans would make an excellent addition to the development committee. He handled his money well and had greatly modernized the farm. Hans at first turned him down. But after some of the other committee members encouraged him, he reluctantly came on board.

John Wesley Fremont graduated from Transparent High School in 1998, just barely. He was the son of the local Methodist minister. During his teenaged years he developed into a fine looking young man with dark, wavy hair and almost black eyes. His always-ready smile revealed a set of perfect teeth. During his freshman and sophomore years he was constantly in trouble and spent an inordinate amount of time in the principal's office. Although they were never able to pin anything on him, he was believed to be into heavy pot smoking and possibly dealing. The girls loved him and he took full advantage of that. Parents of Transparent High girls would gasp in agony if they learned that their daughters had been seen talking with John Wesley, or, heaven forbid, had been seen in his car with him.

In an attempt to make sure he did not flunk out of high school completely, the principal, Charlie Seckman, had moved him into the vocational segment of the curriculum during the middle of his junior year. To everyone's complete surprise, it soon became very evident that John Wesley had good building skills. Charlie Seckman breathed a sigh of relief when John Wesley walked across the stage in the school gymnasium and picked up his diploma. His grade point average was 2.06. When the principal extended his right hand for the traditional congratulatory handshake, John Wesley just reached and patted the shorter man on his bald head. "Stay Loose, Charlie," said John Wesley.

Not long after graduation, John Wesley left for Florida where he got a job with a contractor who was involved in creating a huge housing development. The contractor quickly realized that he had a highly skilled man on his hands. It wasn't long until John Wesley was supervising a large construction crew. In a few months John Wesley was making more money than he ever imagined.

In April of 2003, John Wesley returned to West Virginia. Bankrolled by his former employer, he began taking steps to form his own construction company. By September, he had jumped through all of the hoops with the state and became a certified builder of homes. The Florida developer soon had John Wesley overseeing the construction of a large housing development in Putnam County.

In 2004, John acquired some property up one of the dark

hollows in Transparent County and began building his own home. He was anxious to impress the folks in Transparent County, most especially, Charlie Seckman.

Sidney Alvin Curtin did not overlook his sudden success. He quickly asked John Wesley to serve on the Committee. John Wesley gleefully accepted.

Alvin Deacon Barger was a Transparent County native. Even though he had acquired a degree in education at Marshall University, he had never taught. Through family connections he became a heavy equipment operator as soon as he graduated from Marshall. He operated a dozer on a strip mine for ten years. Deacon had worked a lot of overtime and had piled up some money in Sidney Curtin's bank. During his 34th year on the planet, Deacon decided that he had "gotten the call." So he quit his regular job, became an independent contractor and began jumping through the hoops required to become an ordained Baptist minister.

After a couple of stints as the minister in some small Baptist churches in other counties, Alvin Barger became the minister of the First Baptist Church in Transparent. He acquired the nickname "Deacon" long before he became a preacher because he had always been, as the locals would say, "powerful religious." Everyone knew that he was an outspoken witness for Jesus Christ. Just about everyone started to refer to him as "Deacon" soon after he graduated from high school.

In addition to being a big, tough guy, Deacon was handsome and well spoken. He had a square-jawed face and a frock of dark curly hair that often fell down over his forehead when he preached. He was blessed with a near-perfect smile that he could turn on when he needed to. After he was ordained, he was rarely seen in public without a suit and tie. In just a few minutes into a sermon, he always had the congregation eating out of his hand.

The Reverend Barger's wife had gotten a little plump in her middle years and her body and taken on that "turnip" look. But she was still a rather attractive lady. They had two daughters, one of whom was a very gifted athlete.

Even though Deacon was a very social man, he preferred to live in isolation. He chose not to live in the Baptist parsonage and remained on his twenty-five acre spread that was located in one of the hollows in Transparent County. Deacon was not a farmer. He just enjoyed living in the isolated, wooded area where he had built his house some ten years before.

The Reverend Barger took his job very seriously and was very visible in the community. He was always at the 4-H and FFA activities delivering the opening prayer or blessing the food. If the local PTO, Lions Club, or Rotary needed someone to speak or bless their meeting, Deacon was always available. He was very diligent about "visiting the sick." There was probably not a more respected or well-liked man in Transparent County than Deacon Barger.

Even though he had not really demonstrated any business or entrepreneurial qualities, Sidney thought his respect in the community entitled him to a seat on the Committee.

No Hit Stalnaker was a living legend in Transparent County. Even though he had lettered in four sports at Transparent High School, his claim to fame was baseball. He had pitched a total of four no hitters during his senior year in high school in 1982. From that time on he was always known as No Hit Stalnaker. No one had ever seen the likes of him and he had gotten all kinds of coverage in the Charleston Gazette.

Several Major League teams had recruited him, but he

chose the Cincinnati Reds. He pitched fairly well in the minor leagues and worked himself up to Triple A in two years. The Reds called him up in August of 1985, but he bombed during his first outing. During three starts with the Reds, he never got past the second inning, so they sent him back down. No Hit decided to give up baseball and come back home.

No Hit was twenty-four years old when he came back. He had already lost most of his hair but still maintained his good looks. He lived a little too well during his stint in the minor leagues, and he was more or less broke when he arrived back on his home turf. He got a job clerking in the local hardware store and was very good at it. The job provided lots of contacts. Even though he had failed to make it to the "big show," Transparent County folks still thought very highly of him. He was, after all, a local legend.

No Hit soon enhanced his status in the county by organizing a little league program. It became an obsession with him. No Hit spent hours of his own time raising money and recruiting coaches for the organization. It was successful beyond his imagination.

During his thirtieth year, he married a young divorcee whom he had met through her two sons who played on his little league team. She was a school teacher who had moved to Transparent County to take an elementary teaching job. For appearance purposes No Hit and his new family joined the First Baptist Church.

When the elections rolled around in 2000, No Hit filed for a seat on the County Commission. He won by a landslide.

There was no doubt in Sidney Curtin's mind that No Hit had to be a member of his Economic Development Committee.

THE FIRST MEETING
JANUARY 7, 2005

As the membership of the Transparent County Economic Development Committee gathered around the table on that cold January evening in 2005, Sydney asked Deacon Barger to offer a prayer. Deacon complied and offered up a superb blessing. Sidney then asked Harold Blaney if he would take some rough minutes. "We don't need a lot of detail, but I think we need some sort of record of what we are about." Harold said that he would be glad to do it.

Sydney then asked each member to make a few comments about the direction of the committee. He told them that he had plenty of ideas of his own, but he was anxious to hear what each member had on his mind.

Harold Blaney spoke first. "Sidney," he said, "as I look around the room I am very impressed with the membership that you have assembled here. However, I am bothered by the fact that there are no women or minorities in the group. I am sure you are all aware of the fact that America is no longer a white, male dominated society. In case you haven't noticed, we have a black man running for president. The University, who writes my check each month, is constantly reminding all of its agents to press for diversity in their communities."

That comment brought Cecil Blyer out of his chair. "That's the dumbest damned thing I ever heard of," he said. "We don't need a bunch of mouthy women on this committee, and where in the hell are we supposed to get a minority? As far as I know, there ain't a one in the whole damned county of any stature. What in hell's name has any of them done that would make us want them on this committee? I guess we could bring one in from New York."

Sidney Curtin was taken aback by Cecil's reactions, but ever the smooth diplomat, Sidney handled it well. "Well, I think Harold makes a good point, but Transparent County is somewhat unique in the scheme of things. When I was putting the committee together, I diligently looked for a possible female member, but I just did not come up with one. In fact, I talked with Gina McCray about serving but she said she didn't think she had time for it and suggested that her husband would be a much better member. Frank was a natural choice anyway."

Wesley Fremont smiled and commented, "The Apostle Paul said to let your women be silent in church."

Everyone turned their heads and looked at Wesley, but he quickly added, "You forget that my daddy is a Methodist preacher." There were subdued smiles around the table.

Sidney struggled ahead. "As far as a minority is concerned, Cecil is on target. Unfortunately, adult minorities are pretty thin in our county. I decided that we did not need a token minority on this committee. I wanted someone who could make a contribution."

"Well, I want the record to show that I made the point," said Harold.

Frank McCray nervously cleared his throat several times before he spoke. "I think we have to look at grants to improve our infrastructure before we can attract any private capital to invest in the county. Of course there is lots of federal money out there if anyone knows how to go after it. We have got to find ways to make our area more attractive for businesses. I just don't think there is any doubt about that. How are we going to attract a manufacturing firm of any kind when we don't have public water in half the county? What's worse, there are just a few areas with three-phase power. I think we need to look for some public grants to develop our infrastructure. I also think it might be wise to employ a county grant writer, someone who has the time and the know how to pursue federal money."

This little speech caused John "Wes" Fremont to break his silence. "That's a goddamned good point, Frank," he said. "I am also concerned about the lay of the land. Hell, they ain't enough level land in the county to build a shithouse, let alone a factory. Seems to me we ought to think about excavating some building sites. I don't know where we would get the money to do that other than to take Frank's suggestion and pursue some grants."

Wes Fremont's soliloquy aroused Deacon Barger. "Now Wesley, I know you have been around the block a few more times than some of us, but I see no need for all of that profanity and bad language when we are discussing something as serious as the future of this county. I think we should all keep our conversation civil." Pressing his teeth together into a grim smile, much the way he did when he made an altar call, Deacon lectured the group about the necessity of cleaning up the image of the county. "You know, this county is viewed by some of our neighboring counties as a haven for drug dealers. We also have something of a reputation for having too many people on government relief. I am of the opinion that no self-respecting business enterprise is going to look our way for a place to start a business until we take some steps to make ourselves more attractive."

"Well shit," said No Hit, ignoring Deacon's lecture about bad language. "How the hell are we going to improve our image if we don't find ways to provide people with something to do besides laying around in the beer halls and smoking pot? It's the lack of employment and destitute condition of some of our people that has brought this negative image down on us. I think that's why Sydney has put this committee together. You know it is going to be difficult to attract new businesses to our county, so I am of the opinion that we need to find ways to help the businesses that are already here to improve and expand. Cecil has got a pretty good lumber business going. Let's try to help him make it bigger and better."

Sidney took in all of their comments and was pleased with what he had heard.

"Gentlemen, I really appreciate your willingness to serve on this committee. I think all of you have made some interesting observations about our county. But there is one important point that I would like to make. The state of West Virginia has never had any capital to work with. Needless to say, without capital it is difficult to initiate any development. Frank's comment about attracting private capital is a good one. I mean, the truth is, West Virginia does not know anything about real money. We just don't have a contingent of billionaires sitting around this state. I guess my point is that if we are going to think big and pursue some really meaningful development, we are going to have to look beyond our borders for investors. I think what we need to do is to try to come up with ideas, ideas that would motivate out-of-state investors to give us a look. Before our next meeting, I would like to ask each of you to try to jot down two or three ideas that you think might perk the interest of some private capital. I will try to do the same." Everyone nodded in agreement

"There is one final point I would like to make. Before the meeting started I overheard someone say that we probably needed some sort of a by-law document. I personally see no need for that. I want this committee to be an informal body, just people with a common cause trying to improve our county.

If we keep it informal, we won't have some government agency breathing down our neck. Is anyone opposed to that?"

Everyone was silent.

"I'd like to make one more comment," said Wes Fremont. "I think you guys need to lighten up a little bit. Hell, you sit around this table like we are all attending a wake. We can make improvements in this county without being so damned serious. Let's have some fun with it. You know down in Florida where I was working everyone seemed a lot happier. People around here are just too damned serious."

There was no response to the statement. Everyone just sort of looked down. Sidney let it settle for a moment and made no comment. They all pulled out their calendars, decided on a new meeting date, and adjourned.

TRANSPARENT COUNTY ECONOMIC DEVELOPMENT COMMITTEE THE FINAL MEETING AUGUST 7, 2008

It was still about ninety-five degrees when the members of the Transparent County Economic Development Committee began filing into the conference room at the bank. Sidney Curtin shook hands with each man before they sat down. He asked Deacon to bless the meeting which he did with much grace.

As Sidney looked around the table he noticed that Hans Jorgenson was not present.

"Anyone heard anything out of Hans?"

"I figure he is in the hayfield," said Harold Blaney, the Extension Agent.

"Well, he hasn't been what I would call a sterling committee member, but I still think he could make a contribution if we could get him into it," Sidney replied.

"He's a good man," Frank McCray added. "I think some of us do not realize what it takes to keep a farm like that going. Old Hans does it all himself. I for one admire him for it."

Everyone nodded in concurrence.

"What about Cecil? Anyone seen him?"

"Hell, he hasn't been here since last winter," said Wesley Fremont. "I think we might as well forget that worthless son-of-a-bitch."

"Easy now, Wesley," said Sidney. "I'm sure he has his reasons for not attending."

"He was supposed to be helping me and No Hit on the woodlot project, but he hardly ever returned our calls," said Deacon Barger.

Sidney figured it was time to move the meeting forward. He also thought it was time for some accolades so he began the meeting by lauding some of the members. "As you all know, Wesley, through some of his contacts in the construction business, has managed to get two sites prepared for possible development out near the edge of the county. We don't have any clients at this time but at least we have something better to offer. And, I am happy to report that Frank and Harold have been working toward getting three-phase power out there. We found out just yesterday that we may get an extension of our water line out to the site. I feel certain that we will attract some business once we get that property up to speed. So gentlemen I think we are making progress. I guess we have to confess that we have not added one free enterprise job to the county payroll as yet, but I knew this was not going to be easy.

Deacon Barger raised his hand. "Well, I'm afraid No Hit and I don't have anything positive to report. We were designated by the Committee to talk with some of the chain restaurant people to see if there was any interest in locating a store here. We have talked to McDonald's, Wendy's, Hardee's, and Burger King. All four of them gave basically the same response. They don't believe we have the population base or the traffic flow to support a fast-food restaurant. I think they are wrong, but they won't budge on the issue."

"Well," said Sidney. "I have mixed feelings about the fast-food chains anyway. They won't employ that many people and if one of them did move in it would probably kill our local, family-owned restaurants."

That comment aroused Wes Fremont. "I know fast-food

restaurants have there down side, but when you are trying to attract new businesses to the county, they make you look a little better. Hell, some of the people from the urban areas don't know how to eat without a McDonald's or a Pizza Hut."

"Yes, I know that's true," Sidney replied, "but it sounds like that's a dead issue. What about the woodlot project?" Sidney inquired. "Any progress there?"

"That looks a little better," said No Hit. There seems to be a lot of interest in it, and we think we have located a possible site. To his credit, Cecil Blyer said he would donate a three-acre plot where folks could bring in the firewood. Now we need to think about how we are going to hire someone to manage the place. The problem is, how are we going to pay such a person until the money from sales starts rolling in?"

"I may be able to work something out with the Small Business Administration," said Sidney. "Perhaps I can work on that next week."

"We have established that there is a very good market for firewood over in the Washington, D.C./Baltimore, Maryland, area," Frank McCray interjected. "Of course, we have some transportation issues. We have got to figure out some way to get the wood over there."

"I think we can work that out," said Sidney. "You know, gentlemen, this may be our best hope in the short run to get some money flowing into the county. No Hit, why don't you and Deacon take a closer look at that property Cecil mentioned and see what needs to be done there. Meantime, I'll see what I can do about getting someone to transport the wood. I'm excited about the possibility of getting this project underway. I mean, we have plenty of firewood in this county, plenty of people who are willing to cut it, and now a possible site to coordinate the activity. Let's all get moving on this."

"I have one more comment," Frank McCray said as he cleared his throat for the twentieth time. "If something doesn't happen to the price of gasoline pretty soon, all of our efforts are going to be for nothing. With the price of both gasoline and diesel fuel running above four dollars a gallon, I don't know how I am going to keep the buses running this fall. Looks to me like something is going to blow in this country, and it's going to blow pretty damned soon. If it does blow, I don't think we are going to be worried about economic development. I think we are going to be worried about hanging on."

Sidney Curtin took the comment under consideration but did not make a response as he began looking over his calendar for the next possible meeting date. "How does September 25th look to you guys? That's a Thursday evening. Can everyone make it, say about 7:00 p.m.?"

"I guess we'll all be here if we can afford the gas," Wesley Fremont said with a smile.

FIRST CITIZEN'S BANK OF TRANSPARENT
AUGUST 14, 2008

On August 14, 2008, four days after the incident at the Go-Mart, Sheriff Clayton McKee, walked into the Transparent Citizen's Bank about 10:00 a.m. Sidney Curtin spotted him as soon as he came through the door and walked out to greet him.

"Clayton, how the hell are you?"

"Well, about normal, I guess, Sidney. How about you?"

"Oh, I'm rollin' right along, looking forward to getting out on the golf course and enjoy some good fall weather."

"Ain't that the truth," said Sheriff McKee. "I'm pretty damned tired of this humidity. What are we going to do about a school superintendent this fall?"

"Well, I've talked to some of the School Board members, and they tell me they are going to move Charlie Seckman into the slot, as least for a time. Charlie has been the principal over at the high school for quite some time. I suspect he's pretty clued in."

"Sounds like a reasonable plan to me," said Clayton. "I for one was afraid that the board would look for some out-of-state wonder boy to run the schools. I guess we will be looking for a new county commissioner too, won't we Sidney?"

"Yes, I guess we will. But with the election coming up in November, I suspect they will limp along with two members until January."

"Speaking of county commissioners, Sidney, I'd like to ask you a few questions."

"Sure," Sidney replied. "Come on in the office."

Clayton McKee had known Sidney for a long time. He had also known his daddy well. When he left the county to join the Navy, Sidney was just a kid. When he came back to Transparent County, Sidney was already working at the bank. Clayton noticed immediately that Sidney had presence. He wasn't sure what it was. Maybe it was those steely blue eyes that he always focused on you when he talked.

"Sidney," Clayton began, "I know that all three of the men who were involved in the big fracas over at the Go-Mart were members of your Economic Development Committee. You probably knew them as well as anyone. I mean, hell, these guys were the backbone of the county in many ways. Did you ever notice any kind of conflict among them?"

"You know, Clayton, I'm sure you are tired of hearing this, but I am still totally perplexed by all of this. Deacon and No Hit exchanged some strong words in the meetings a time or two, but they always appeared to be friends when the meeting ended. I certainly didn't observe anything that would have led to such an attack. The two of them have been working on getting a woodlot established in the county so I know they have been in contact outside the meetings. The last time we met back on August 7, they appeared to be getting along just fine. That was just two days before the incident. I don't know what the hell could have happened to set Deacon off between Thursday evening and Saturday morning. And Frank McCray, for Christ's sake, he was the quiet man on the Committee. And you know, Clayton, Frank was not even a hunter. I don't think I ever heard him mention a gun. I didn't even know he owned one."

"Well, he did have a permit to carry a concealed weapon. It's on file at my office, but that don't tell me a damned thing.

Just about every male in the county and half of the females have one of those."

"Do you have any leads at all, Clayton? Anything to go on?"

"No, I'm sorry to say at this point, I am clueless. I have no idea why Deacon would batter No Hit, and I certainly have no idea why Frank would want to shoot Deacon. There must be a connection there somewhere but I'm damned if I know where it is."

"Have you talked with the widows yet? Maybe they know something."

"I have talked to Deacon's wife and to Gina McCray. Both of those conversations led to a dead end. I have not talked with No Hit's wife. I thought I would give her a little time."

"That's good of you, Clayton. You know some of your critics say you are too full of the milk of human kindness to be sheriff," Sidney said with a smile.

"Well, that may be true, but I can be mean enough when I have to," said Clayton as he got out of his chair. "If you stumble across anything, Sidney, I'd appreciate it if you would give me a call. I guess you'll be going down to the Memorial Service in the morning won't you?"

"Yes, I plan to attend. How about you?"

"I'll be down there for sure. I'll have to help out with the traffic."

As soon as Clayton left Sidney's office, one of his vice presidents, Harley McCourt, came in with a letter and handed it to Sidney.

"Looks like we are going to have some federal auditors poking around in a couple of weeks, Sidney. I don't know if it's routine or if something's gone awry."

Sidney cleared his throat nervously. "We've had them

in here before so I guess we can handle it, Harley. I'll call a meeting in a couple of days and we'll get prepared."

Sidney Curtin was not only the president of the bank; he was really the president of the county. He had never held an elective office but most folks agreed that he called the shots. If the county commission came up with a plan to spend a substantial amount of the county's money, one of them always went to the bank and "ran it by Sidney" before any official action was taken. Or if Frank McCray, the highly paid Superintendent of Schools, wanted to make a major move of any kind, he not only had to get it by the Board of Education, but he also had to "run it by Sidney." Even Harold Blaney, the Extension Agent, always let Sidney know what he was doing, especially if it involved taking kids out of the county. That's just the way things were and everybody accepted it.

But Sidney carried it all off very well. He never appeared arrogant. Yet no important personnel appointment ever got made in Transparent County without Sidney's approval. He was always consulted and had been known to veto a few. In fact, the Board of Education had held a secret meeting in the bank conference room after Frank McCray skipped town. Some of the board members wanted to go "out of the county" and hire a professional to run the schools. But Sidney informed them that Charlie Seckman would be his choice.

"Charlie is a local boy, is familiar with the system, and is very capable," Sidney declared when it came his turn to speak. "I don't see how we could go wrong with him."

When the Transparent County Board of Education met the next evening, Charlie got the job.

Yet everyone liked Sidney Curtin. He was always out in the lobby of the bank during working hours, shaking hands and talking with his "friends and neighbors."

He was also a very wise banker and very careful with loan money. Sidney was never a man to turn down a reasonably good risk, but he would turn down a bad risk in a minute. The bank had the reputation of being one of the "soundest banks in the nation." The majority of the shares in the bank were held by local people. The local car dealer financed all of his wholesale purchases at the bank, but he was also a major stockholder. There were rumors that the Wall Street banks might come crashing down in the near future, but no one was worried about their money in Sidney's bank.

The biggest criticism of Sidney and his wife, Mary Beth, was that they did not attend church. Some of the fundamental preachers had even confronted him a time or two about his lack of church attendance. Sidney always defended himself with the same explanation. Churches, he would tell his critics, are a good thing. They serve a very useful purpose for some people. But then he would tell them very directly that he just never felt the need for a public display of his religious convictions. "I often talk with God up under a big white-oak tree on the farm," he would say without a smile. "I'm a firm believer and God and I have an understanding. In my mind, religion is a spiritual thing, church is a social thing."

He also took some heat for not attending any of the public school athletic events. Even though his bank sometimes funded special trips by the athletic teams, Sidney had absolutely no interest in sports, except for golf. But ballgames were the most significant social events that happened. Friday night football games brought everybody out whether they were interested in the game or not. Like many of the socialites in the urban areas who attended parties, they came to the football games to be seen. But Sidney refused to play that game. He once remarked that he had no intention of sitting on a cold bleacher board for three hours in late October to watch an event that held no interest for him. Since he and Mary Beth had no children, he felt no need to go.

Sidney was very devoted to Mary Beth. Many powerful men become convinced that they are special and can have all of the women they want and still keep their wives. But that was not within Sidney's character. He always felt like he was fortunate to have married such a wonderful woman.

But Sidney did have one flaw. He loved to gamble and he wasn't very good at it.

It started with the dog track at Cross Lanes. He started visiting the track on Saturday nights and betting on the dogs during the summer of 2005. He never won anything, but he didn't mind. Sometimes he would hang around after the races and play the slots.

He was not much of a drinking man but every now and then he would stop by the bar and have a beer before he drove home. One evening during the summer of 2006 while he was enjoying a beer, a man approached him and stuck out his hand. "You're Mr. Curtin, aren't you, president of the bank over in Transparent County?"

"That's right," Sidney replied. "I don't believe I have had the pleasure."

"I'm Blackey Malcome," he smiled. "I run a construction company down in Putnam County. I've seen you around the casino many times and finally asked someone who you were. You obviously like to gamble a little, but I was wondering if you are a poker player?"

"Not really," Sidney replied. "I used to love to play for pennies when I was in college, but I haven't played much since then. I do know the rules, though."

"I just wanted to let you know, said Blackey Malcome, "that there's a fairly high stakes game that goes on in Putnam County about once a month. One of the players is a bank president, like you. The others are business leaders. It's a pretty well-heeled crowd, usually four or five of us. We're always interested in new blood. I just wanted to extend you an invitation. If you would ever like to join us, just give me a call. Here is my card."

"Thanks," Sidney replied, as he accepted the card. "I'll think about it."

About a week later Sidney decided that he would go down one night and just watch. But he stuck a thousand dollars in his pocket just in case he was tempted to get in. He followed the directions provided by Mr. Malcome and found himself pulling up into the driveway of a very expensive looking house. Mr. Malcome met him outside and took him into the basement of the house. They went into a room with a very professional looking poker table. He was introduced to four prosperous looking gentlemen.

After the introductions, Sidney told them that he would just like to watch the first evening because it had been a while since he had played. They all smiled and gave their approval. But once Sidney watched them play a few rounds of five-card draw and seven- card stud, he couldn't stand it. He purchased five hundred dollars worth of chips and took a seat at the table. He lost the five hundred in about an hour and a half. He bought another five hundred dollars' worth and was able to stay in the game until they stopped at 11:00 p.m. When he got home he figured out that he had lost about $850 bucks. But, he had had a hell of a good time.

Sidney returned to the poker game nearly every month and was a heavy loser just about every time. In fact, he began to worry that Mary Beth was going to notice the disappearance of their money. He had never told her he was in the poker clan. He just continued to tell her that he was going down to Cross Lanes. Mary Beth trusted him so completely that she never once questioned him about his whereabouts.

During all of his years working at the bank, Sidney had thought many times about how easy it would be to pull some of the bank's money into his personal account. He had never really tried to do it, but he was pretty sure there were a couple of fool-proof ways. He was very adept on the computer and fully understood the system the bank utilized.

One Monday evening in October of 2006 he decided to stay at the bank after everyone left and look into it. He knew what auditors looked for, so he figured all he had to do was disguise a few transfers. When he left the bank that evening, there was an extra $5,850 in his personal account.

In the back of his mind he thought that if he hit a good winning streak in the game, he would put the money back and no one would be the wiser. He had seen a couple of the players leave the game with more than five thousand in winnings. But Sidney kept losing. He would sometimes just about break even, but he was never a big winner. After about six months of losing and shifting money in his bank, he became more and more convinced that no one was ever going to figure out what he was doing with his account transfer scheme. So he began to play with larger numbers.

Before long he was playing with six figures. Then a strange thing happened. Now that he did not have to worry about how much he would lose, he became a better poker player. But he never got around to replacing any of the money that he had fleeced from the bank.

Sidney wasn't really scared about the federal auditors coming to town, just a little nervous.

THE EULOGIES

The service for Reverend Barger had been conducted at the First Baptist Church. The church did not begin to hold the well-wishers, not to mention the curious. The same situation occurred when the service for No Hit Stalnaker was held at the local funeral home. Only a tiny fraction of those in attendance were able to get inside.

County officials, with the overwhelming support of the community, decided to have a joint memorial service for the two men at the high school gymnasium on Saturday afternoon, August 16. People began arriving just after noon for the 2:00 p.m. affair. They gathered in small groups in front of the high school. It was apparent that most of the people came in support of No Hit. Conversations were laced with comments such as, "I have never seen anyone who could send the ball up to the plate like he could." Some of those who had played against him in high school drove many miles to pay their respects. One of them was overheard remarking, "I was never able to even hit the ball. He struck me out every time. The boy had mustard on the ball, not doubt about it."

Still, the Reverend Barger had his supporters in the crowd. He had endeared himself to many county residents by sitting with them when their loved ones were in their final hours. He had also been a big supporter of youth groups such as 4-H and Boy Scout troops. As a result, many of the young folks in the county had gotten to know him whether they had gone to his church or not. Many of those young folks were now adults. One of the young men in the crowd was overheard saying that

Reverend Barger was "what a preacher ought to be."

It was hot inside the non-air-conditioned gymnasium. The hot and humid weather pattern that had started in early August was hanging on. The folding chairs that had been arranged on the gym floor filled quickly because it was a little cooler down on the floor. Yet, just about every space in the bleachers was occupied.

The Reverend Erwin Boone from the First Methodist Church of Transparent presided over the service. Reverend Boone was far and away Transparent County's most educated and sophisticated preacher. He had been in the county for only two years.

Boone led the opening prayer and briefly eulogized each man. He covered the area that had stirred the curiosity of most of those in attendance. "No one in this room knows what series of events led to the tragic ending of these two fine men," he said. "As the size of this gathering indicates, they were both highly regarded. Perhaps some day, we will know. And if and when we do learn about the circumstances, our opinions might be altered. But right now, all we know is we have lost two good community leaders. They were both good Christian men. We pray that God will have mercy on their souls."

He then proceeded to introduce an array of speakers. Some of them spoke too long. You could see the disapproval in the audience as many of those in the bleachers pulled at their collars and shifted around on the hard boards. Other speakers became emotional and could hardly get through their spiel. Oftentimes at memorial services speakers will relate humorous stories about the deceased. Such was not the case at this particular service.

The speaker who got the most attention was a gentleman by the name of Delbert Roddy. He spoke in glowing terms about what No Hit had done for the young people in the county. "It was through his efforts, and his efforts alone that we have such a successful Little League program in our county. He put in endless hours of his time putting the program together. In retrospect, some of us should have helped him more. I know he struggled mightily, just trying to raise the money to get things started. I don't think any of us appreciated that enough. We will never replace No Hit. We will just have to learn to live without him."

His comments aroused a few "Amen's" in the crowd.

Eighty-year-old Mary Baldwin delivered by far the most emotional presentation. She spoke for a few minutes in rather civil tones about what a good man the Reverend was. Then she began to wail and cry as she spoke. "How could Frank McCray shoot such a man?" she moaned. "Why would he do such a thing? Surely God will seek him out and bring His fury down on him."

When she finally settled down, there were a few cries of "Well glory," and "Bless her Lord, Bless her good."

It was interesting to note that the Revered Barger's wife was not in attendance. No Hit's wife sat in an honored place near the temporary platform that held the speakers. Every speaker alluded to her in one way or another. Gina McCray, wife of the shooter at the Go-Mart affair, was also not in attendance.

Sheriff McKee and Sidney Curtin sat on the front row together and took it all in. Sheriff McKee was not quite sure what he thought about the entire affair. His only conclusion was that people sometimes put a strange twist on things. Here they were, making a hero out of a man who took a baseball bat and beat another man to death.

TRANSPARENT COUNTY SHERIFF'S OFFICE
SEPTEMBER 22, 2008

Sheriff Clayton McKee had lots of pressing responsibilities. He had to spend time in both the Magistrate Court and the Circuit Court. Due to some resignations, he currently had only two deputies. One deputy had abruptly resigned and taken a job with the Charleston, West Virginia, Police Department. Another one had gotten caught selling some pain pills that he had confiscated from a man he had arrested. As a result the sheriff found himself serving subpoenas and performing other routine duties that his office required. A little more than a month had slipped by since the awful scene at the Go-Mart. The truth was he had not devoted much time to the investigation of the crime. But he thought about it all the time. So far, he had made absolutely no progress. He wondered why the media had not pursued the story much. There was a big splash in the Charleston papers right after the fact. He had been interviewed a couple of times by both newspaper reporters and by the area television stations. But he had not heard a word out of any of them for about three weeks. It was fast becoming a cold case.

It occurred to him that it had been more than a month since his talk with Sidney Curtin. He had not followed up on his plan to talk with each member of the Transparent County Economic Development Committee. The West Virginia State Police had also assigned a man to the case but it appeared that all of his efforts were being devoted to finding Frank McCray. He had been by the office a couple of times, but it was obvious that the officer did not know any more about Frank's whereabouts than the sheriff did. Clayton not only wanted to find Frank McCray, he wanted to know what the hell brought the situation on in the first place.

This warm Monday morning found Clayton sitting at his desk looking at a list of the membership of the Committee. He picked up a pencil and underlined each name carefully. Three of them were gone; two murdered, and the other had disappeared. He put a checkmark beside Sidney's name. He felt like he needed to talk with each surviving member. Maybe, just maybe, one of them would provide something to go on. He settled on Cecil Blyer for his next interview. He knew Cecil only by sight, had never talked with him. All he knew about him was that he had a pretty successful lumber business. He had never met his wife, wasn't even sure if he had one.

Clayton drove over to the sawmill about ten miles out of town. He spotted Cecil up on a stack of lumber with some kind of a pole in his hand. He was shifting boards around. The sheriff approached the lumber pile.

"Good morning, Mr. Blyer," he ventured. "If you could spare a few minutes, I would like to ask you a couple of questions."

Cecil jumped down off the lumber and walked toward Clayton. "What the hell you want to talk to me about? I ain't done nothin' and I've paid my taxes," he said without a smile.

Clayton sized him up a little before he spoke again. He observed his thick neck and powerful shoulders. The sheriff had been in a few fistfights in his life. He knew how to evaluate an opponent. Cecil Blyer was one of those guys you could hit in the head all day and never faze him. "I'm just trying to make heads or tails out of the beating and shooting that took place over at the Go-Mart. I know that you served on the Economic Development Committee with all three of the men who were involved. I just wondered if you might have noticed anything transpiring among the three of them."

"Hell, I don't know nothin' about any of 'em," Cecil replied. "I hardly ever had any contact with them except at the meetings. Frank McCray seemed like a pretty good feller, but I didn't care much for No Hit or that jackleg preacher. Course, I was real sorry to hear that they got killed. But I ain't got no idea why they would have been fussin' about something. I missed the last meeting so I ain't seen none of 'em for a while."

The sheriff studied Cecil for thirty seconds or so and thought to himself, *What an asshole! I guess he's living proof of the fact that you don't have to be a nice guy or have a college education to be successful.*

"I appreciate your time," said Sheriff McKee as he stuck out his hand.

Cecil Blyer just turned around and walked off.

No one really knew much about Cecil Blyer. Sidney Curtin did not look into his background at all when he asked him to serve on the Committee. He just based the invitation on Cecil's business success. There was a dark side of Cecil that no one knew about.

During one of his timber jobs, just a few miles from his place, Cecil became aware of a young girl who lived with her family in an old two story farmhouse. The house had been abandoned at one time. The current resident had shored the old place up a little, but it was still in bad shape. Cecil noticed that there were places where you could see daylight through the walls. The family consisted of a man and his wife and four children. They were welfare all the way. The girl he had noticed was a pretty, good-looking kid and kept herself presentable. She was seventeen years old and had quit school at the end of her sophomore year.

One summer evening at the end of his workday, as Cecil was putting his tools into his pickup, he spotted her walking along the road. He got into his truck and eased it along until he caught up with her. He pulled off the road just ahead of her and got out. She kept coming toward him and did not change her expression, nor did she acknowledge his presence as she passed him by.

"You're not a very friendly sort, are you?" he said with a half smile.

"I don't know you," she replied.

"I'm Cecil Blyer," he said. "I live just a few miles away. Been work'n on this timber job for a few weeks."

"Yes," she said without a smile. "I've seen you coming and going."

"Do you have a boyfriend?" he asked crudely.

"Not a steady one," she replied.

"Would you go out with an older man?" he asked.

"How old are you?" she inquired. "You don't look very old."

"I just turned twenty-six. What are you? Bout fifteen?"

"I'm seventeen, be eighteen in a couple of weeks," she replied, still not smiling. "I just might go out with you. Why don't you stop by the house this Saturday and we'll see."

"Do you have a name," he ventured.

"I am Fannie Mae Conner," she replied.

Cecil stopped by her house as instructed. It wasn't long until he and Fannie Mae began a courtship of sorts. The first time he picked her up, he stopped at a convenience store and picked up a twelve pack of beer. Cecil drove up a hollow where he knew no one lived, pulled down by the creek and parked. They talked until dark, mostly about how she had hated school and how all of the snooty town girls looked down on her. He drank ten beers; she drank two. He made no attempt to touch her.

When he stopped in front of her house to let her out, she opened her door and looked at him with a sly look.

"What are you, one of them gay boys? You didn't even try to kiss me."

He reached across the seat of the pickup, grabbed her by the neck and pulled her back inside. She sat silently by his side as he roared down the dirt road until he came to a wide place. He pulled off the road and attacked her brutally, tearing at her clothes and smothering her with kisses. She put up no resistance. Afterwards, he gave her time to dress and drove her back to her house. She opened the door and looked at him.

"I guess you are not one of them gay boys after all. That was quite a tussle."

Three weeks later, Fannie Mae moved into the mobile home with Cecil. They did not even discuss marriage. Cecil went to work every morning, leaving her alone. She kept house a little bit and tried to get him something to eat when he came home. Cecil soon discovered that he was a far better cook and assumed most of the kitchen chores. She nagged at him until he finally bought her a television and hooked it to a small satellite.

Once the TV was installed, Fannie Mae spent her days watching the daytime soaps and eating potato chips. Despite her persistent requests, he still would not have a phone installed.

Cecil was a very strong and vigorous man and it was a rare evening when they did not have a prolonged sexual tryst. Fannie Mae enjoyed it as much as he did and never put up any resistance. In fact, she started many of the sessions. Three months after she moved in, she realized she was pregnant. That's when her life started to get more complicated.

First, she began to think about a last name for her child. Would it be Blyer or Conner? Cecil showed absolutely no interest in the coming blessed event. He had never once mentioned marriage and she was hesitant to raise the issue. When she finally did get up the nerve to broach the subject, he dismissed it with a shrug. But she persisted and kept reminding Cecil that the child needed a legal name. Finally, he exploded into a rage.

"No, goddamn it, I ain't getting married. Get married and the next thing you know we will be in divorce court and you'll be suing me for child support and trying to take everything I own."

Fannie was stunned. She had never heard him speak so harshly. In fact, he had become an almost entirely different person since she told him she was expecting. It was almost like he resented her presence. She decided to wait for a while before she brought the subject of marriage up again. Perhaps he would begin to feel differently as the pregnancy progressed.

Then she started to have fits of nausea at different hours of the day. With her, it was not morning sickness. It could happen anytime. Even though she was a regular coffee drinker, she got so she could not even stand the smell of it. Most evenings, when she sat down to supper, she would gag on the first bite.

Although Cecil's sexual appetite did not wane, she just tolerated the sessions. She was very aware of the fact that she was not responding properly to his advances but she was just not interested. Love making became an almost daily chore that she had to endure. At first, he did not say anything, but he would often retreat to the porch afterwards and pull on a bottle of whiskey until he was in a stupor. Most mornings he would leave for work without saying a word to her.

One late fall evening, during her sixth month of pregnancy, she heard him slide into the driveway and slam the door on the pickup. She looked out the window and realized that he was very drunk. He leaned against the truck for a minute or two before coming inside. When he came through the door, she saw that his eyes were glassy. He stared at her for a few seconds; then bellowed out in a tone she had never heard him use.

"I'm tired of you treating me like a goddamn dog. Now you get every stitch of your clothes off and get your sloppy ass in the bed. You hear me?"

Fannie was terrified. She was afraid to resist him, but she was also concerned about her child. It was hard to tell what he would do to her considering his state.

"Not now, Cecil," she replied meekly. "Why don't you settle down a little and I'll take you to bed later."

"Settle down, hell," he said. "I've been settled down for weeks and you are about like fuckn' a bag of marshmallows. I've had it with you. Now get your ass in the bedroom."

"Not now, Cecil. I'm afraid you will hurt the baby or me. Sit down, and I will make you come coffee."

The back of his right hand caught her in the corner of her right eye. The blow turned her head sideways. Then both of his open hands caught her in the chest and knocked her backwards. She hit the floor on her butt, then her head went backwards, and she was flat on her back. She rolled over and tried to crawl under the kitchen table. But he grabbed her by the ankles and pulled her back. He grasped both her shoulders and jerked her to her feet. Laura screamed, but there was no one to hear in that dark hollow.

He picked her up and carried her to the bedroom. Cecil literally tore her clothes from her body and flung her onto the bed.

"If you don't want me to hurt your precious baby, get over on your stomach. He approached her from behind and drove himself into her with such force that she screamed and cried for mercy. But her cries went unheeded and he continued his ravage. When he finished, he got dressed and left her sobbing on the bed. She heard him start his truck and roar down the dirt road.

Cecil did not return to the trailer that night, or the next day. Fannie had no phone. Her nearest neighbors were about a mile away and she had never met any of them. Her family was about four miles away. After Cecil did not return on the second day, she decided she had better walk the four miles and tell her mother what had happened.

Before Cecil came into her life, she often went for long walks so it was no major challenge for her.

Her mother and dad did not have much to say after she explained how her relationship with Cecil had crashed. They just advised her that she had better stay with them. They all agreed that it might not be safe for her to return to the trailer. Her dad drove back around and picked up what few belongings she had.

Even though she was in her sixth month, Fannie had not consulted a doctor about her pregnancy. Her mother took her to the county clinic and got her on a pre-natal schedule with one of the doctors who took care of welfare clients.

Just when she was about to get used to the fact that she was going to have a baby with no father and no last name, Cecil drove up into the yard one evening and blew the horn on his truck. Fannie drew back the curtain in the kitchen and saw him getting out. She reluctantly and fearfully walked out to meet him.

He began to apologize for being mean to her and laid his

behavior onto the liquor he had been drinking. He asked her to move back in with him. He even suggested that maybe they would go down to the courthouse in a week or so and see about getting married. He said that he had wanted to come by before, but just could not face her.

Fannie went back into the house, picked up a few things, and rode back to the trailer with Cecil. He was very kind to her when they arrived and told her that he would not expect any sex until after the baby came. Fannie carefully tried to explain to him that they should probably wait for the baby to come before they got married. Otherwise, he would have to assume all of the doctor's bills. He readily agreed to those terms. Cecil also told her that he would get a telephone installed so she could call her mother if she needed her for anything. He also worried that she may need to call her doctor.

Fannie Mae was never sure what brought about the change in Cecil, but during the following months, he had been a perfect gentleman. Soon after the baby came, they got married and Cecil began building a nice house right next to the trailer. But shortly after the house was completed, Cecil came home one evening with liquor on his breath. When Fannie Mae asked him if he had been drinking, he flew into a rage and ended up slapping her across the mouth. He stopped after the first slap and seemed very remorseful. But Fannie Mae learned to always be wary of him after he had been drinking. She accepted the fact that there was a streak of violence in him and tried very hard not to offend him.

TRANSPARENT COUNTY COURTHOUSE
OCTOBER 2, 2008

September had come and gone. Sheriff McKee had still made no progress on the Frank McCray case. Nor had he had any reports at all from the NCIC. The only report he had received that was the least bit helpful was a call from the Hertz rental car people that the Ford Focus had been found in a hotel parking lot in New York City. So he knew Frank did not drive to Florida. That narrowed the field of play down to the other forty-nine states and the District of Columbia.

As so often happens in such cases, things grow cold very quickly when the suspect is not in the vicinity. The sheriff kept hoping that he would get a call that Frank had been picked up somewhere. He concluded that he would devote what time he could to trying to figure out a motive.

He had talked with No Hit's wife and found out absolutely nothing that would help him. She told him that her husband and Deacon had appeared to be good friends. She said that No Hit often talked about Anita, the reverend's daughter, and what a talented athlete she was. Mrs. Stalnaker also said that No Hit had mentioned to her a time or two that he did not think Anita's parents took enough interest in their daughter's games. He said that her mother came to the games on an irregular basis and Deacon rarely attended.

All of that was interesting to the sheriff, but there was nothing in the conversation that gave him any reason why Deacon would just up and beat the preacher to death with a ball bat. Despite his best efforts, the sheriff had not been able to tie the three men together in any way. He was beginning to think that there was no connection. He was beginning to think that Deacon had attacked No Hit for some reason that had nothing to do with Frank McCray. For the life of him, he could not fit Frank into the story.

He had not yet talked with Hans Jorgenson, Wes Fremont, and Harold Blaney, the other three members of the Transparent County Economic Development Committee. Somehow, he doubted if any of them would be of any help, but he decided that he should probably at least give it a try. That was one thing he had learned during his eight years as sheriff. Sometimes the key to solving a case would come from where you least expected it.

He did not know Hans Jorgenson. He had seen him many times, but the word around town was that the Jorgensons were a strange bunch, so he had sort of put off talking with Hans. Wes Fremont was going to be a hard man to track down. He was busy with a big building project in Putnam County. Also, the sheriff had heard that he spent weekends in Florida. He remembered Wes well when he was in high school and he knew his family. But he had had no contact at all with him since he built his big house. He knew Harold Blaney pretty well. The Extension Office was in the annex next to the courthouse so he often bumped into Harold during the course of the day. Harold was a very friendly, outgoing guy. Clayton decided that asking him some questions would be at least a pleasant experience. But there were a few things about the Extension Agent that the sheriff did not know.

After Harold Blaney had been in town for a few months, word got around that he knew a lot about livestock and vegetable gardens, so he started to get several offers to make house calls to look at a sick cow, or perhaps render some advice on how to prevent tomato blight. Many times he was invited into the house for a cup of coffee or a glass of tea. Harold always accepted the offer. He was the sort of guy who was comfortable with just about anyone, regardless of their social class or station in life. He had been to Sidney Curtin's house on a couple of occasions as well as some of the homes of other members of the Economic Development Committee.

During the summer of 2006, Harold got a call from a Mrs. Sebolt. She told him something was destroying her cabbage and broccoli plants and she wondered if he might come down and take a look at them. Harold figured he knew what the problem was and could have told her what to do about it over the phone, but it was a pretty morning, so he decided to drive out and take a look.

He found the Sebolt place without difficulty. He walked up on the porch and knocked on the door. He was greeted by a very attractive woman, probably in her mid-thirties, who invited him inside. Harold accepted and found himself inside a very well-kept and attractive interior.

"Before you look at my garden, how about a cup of coffee?' she offered.

It was about mid-morning and a cup of coffee sounded pretty good to Harold. They walked into her kitchen where she poured them both a cup. They made extended eye contact as she sat down across the table from him.

"My husband works in Charleston," she said. "He leaves early and gets home late, so the garden is pretty much my baby. I do pretty well but don't know squat about insecticides. I put some Seven on the cabbage, but it didn't seem to make any difference. The funny thing is, I don't see any bugs on the plants. Yet something just keeps eating the leaves."

Harold had taken a glance at the garden as he came into the yard but did not get close enough to make an analysis. He did notice she had a very poorly constructed electric fence around it to keep the deer out.

"We'll take a look when we finish our coffee," he said. His curiosity was aroused a little bit as he looked around the house. He didn't see any pictures of kids or any toys scattered about.

"Do you have kids?' Harold asked. "I'm just curious."

"No," she replied. "It's just Ed and me. He never wanted children."

"That's interesting," Harold replied. "I never had any either, but it was my wife who didn't want any. I always thought it would be nice to have a couple. I think kids keep people from being so selfish."

Mrs. Sebolt only smiled. It was a very pretty smile.

"Let's go out and take a look at that cabbage," said Harold. "Perhaps I can help."

When Harold got to where he could see the cabbage and broccoli, his suspicions were confirmed. He knelt down to take a closer look.

"I think what you have here, Mrs. Sebolt, is a rabbit problem. I noticed that you have only one strand of electric fence around the garden. That will keep out the deer, but not the rabbits. They don't seem to be bothering anything else, so if I were you, I would just get me some three-foot chicken wire and put it around the cabbage and broccoli. Rabbits are usually fairly easy to discourage with a fence unless they see a way to squeeze under. Have you not seen any rabbits during the evenings?"

"No, I haven't noticed any, but I do most of my gardening during the early morning hours. I tend to stay in the air conditioning during the warm evenings. I'm afraid I'm not much of a fence builder," she said. "I had a terrible time trying to get that strand of electric wire up to keep the deer out. As you can see, I didn't do a very good job.

"What about your husband? Wouldn't he do it for you?"

"Oh, I doubt it," she replied. "He gets home so late and he really has very little interest in the garden. Weekends, he likes to play golf."

Harold digested all of that for a minute before he replied.

"Well," he said, "if you will get about a dozen four foot metal stakes and some chicken wire, I'll come down and do it for you."

"Oh, I wouldn't want you to do that," she replied. "You are probably not supposed to do that kind of stuff in your job. I guess I can get it up some way."

"Well, that's one of the good things about being an Extension Agent," said Harold. "My boss is in far away Morgantown, so I can do about what I want to. I figure my job is to help make life easier for people, so that's what I do. You get the supplies and give me a call. I'll do the fence."

As she walked out to the car with him, Harold gave her a good long look. He liked what he saw.

Next morning his phone rang soon after he arrived at the office. It was Mrs. Sebolt.

"I have the fence and the stakes," she said. "Whenever you get time, just come on down. I plan to be around all week."

Harold told his secretary that he had to go look at a garden and was soon sitting in Mrs. Sebolt's kitchen enjoying another cup of coffee. They went out to the garden together, and in no time at all Harold had constructed a little rabbit-proof fence around Mrs. Sebolt's plants. She thanked him profusely as she walked toward his car with him. Harold put the little sledge hammer and a couple of pairs of pliers that he had brought with him into the trunk of his car. As he turned around, he and

Mrs. Sebolt exchanged a long stare.

"You know," he said, "I don't even know your first name, but you know mine. That's not hardly fair, is it?"

She smiled and continued her stare.

"I'm Ruby," she said.

"The name fits you perfectly," Harold responded, as he started to slide under the wheel of his car.

She touched his arm gently as if she wanted him to pause. He turned and met her stare again.

"You know, Harold," I have really enjoyed meeting you and talking with you." She hesitated a moment and looked down at the ground. "If you ever find yourself out of something to do some morning, why don't you give me a call and come by for a cup of coffee. There's no harm in that, is there?"

"I'd say not," he replied. "I, too, have enjoyed getting acquainted. You sure you wouldn't mind if I dropped by?"

"Not at all," she said. "You come by anytime."

Harold became a regular visitor at the Sebolt household. One morning she told him that she could not get her lawn mower started and wondered if he would take a look at it. They walked to the back of her garage where the mower was located. Harold pulled the cord a couple of times. The mower did not fire. Harold noticed that it was an older mower without a priming bubble. He took the air filter off the carburetor and pulled the cord again. He noticed that there was no gas squirting in. He took her gas can and poured in a dab of gasoline and pulled the cord again. The mower took off.

"It just needed primed a little," said Harold. "Sometimes after they sit around for a while, they'll act like that."

"Well, aren't you clever," said Ruby.

Harold put the cover back on the air filter and shut the mower down. When he stood up, Ruby was standing very close to him looking him right in the eye. Before he hardly knew what happened, he had her in his arms, kissing her breath away. He was not sure he had ever been that thrilled with a kiss. He hated to let her go. When he did finally step back, she smiled a very broad smile.

"Come on into the house." she said quietly.

They both soon agreed that Harold would have to quit stopping by on a regular basis. Her house was located along the main road and was too conspicuous. Someone would figure out what was going on. Harold told her that folks put two and two together and he did not want to risk losing his job, or causing problems for her.

But they were victims of a passion too strong to be denied. They started meeting at Harold's house. Or, sometimes she would meet him in Charleston or Morgantown. They were very careful never to be seen together. Even though they were very discreet and careful, some rumors had surfaced about their relationship. But neither of them were aware of the rumors. Neither was Sheriff McKee.

It was the second of October when the sheriff walked into the Extension Office to question the agent. Harold's very attractive secretary, Judy Sharp, greeted him. Even though she was twenty-three and Sheriff McKee was seventy-one, he often flirted with her when he saw her around the courthouse. She was cute and bouncy and always had a complimentary remark to make to just about everyone. She was always telling the sheriff that he was cute for a man his age.

"Why, Sheriff McKee," she said as he entered the office, "I've been wondering when you were going to come and see me. I think you have been neglecting me."

"I haven't meant to," the sheriff responded. "You just have so many men around you all the time that I can't edge my way in."

They both shared a good laugh.

"Actually, Judy, I dropped by to talk with your boss. Is he in today?"

"You know, sheriff, I think he is out in the parking lot working on his truck. At least that's where he said he was going."

"Thanks, Judy. I'll go out and take a look. You and I are going to have to visit more often."

"You know where I am," she teased.

Sheriff McKee walked out to the parking lot beside the courthouse annex and saw Harold Blaney's feet and legs sticking out from under the rear end of his Chevy Silverado. Clayton knelt down and peered under at him.

"What the hell you doing under there, Harold, stealing gasoline?"

Harold wriggled out from under the truck, stood up and brushed his hands together.

"No, as I recall from my youth, sheriff, you can do that with a hose without getting under the truck.

Clayton laughed. "You know I did a little of that too when I was young. We used to steal it out of state-road trucks. We called it the Oklahoma Credit Card."

They both laughed.

"Actually, Clayton, I was working on a wiring harness so I can hook up a new utility trailer I bought the other day. Every now and then I need one to haul some big stuff around."

"They're a handy thing to have around," said the sheriff. "Sometimes I wish I had one."

"What can I do for you today?" Harold asked. "It's almost too late in the year for garden questions. You got a sick cow or something?"

"No, if you have a few minutes I'd like to ask you a few questions about the Frank McCray shooting."

"I doubt that I can help you, but fire away," said Harold as he put his arms over the bed of the truck so he could lean a little.

"I guess you knew all three of the guys involved in the fracas pretty well?"

"You know, sheriff, I really didn't know any of them much except for Frank himself.

Frank and I worked on some grants together. Then, of course, I always had several in-school 4-H programs going and we sometimes had to talk about those. I had very little contact with No Hit, and even less with Reverend Barger."

"Did you ever notice any friction between any of them?" Sheriff McKee asked.

"No, not really. But you know No Hit and the preacher were cut from totally different cloth. No Hit was one of those carefree, easy-going guys. He seemed to enjoy life to the fullest. And the preacher, well, he took life pretty seriously. They clashed sometimes when the Committee met. But I never saw anything that would indicate to me that either of them wanted to bring harm to the other."

"What about Deacon's daughter, Anita? Do you know her?"

"Sure do. She is in the 4-H program and has been to camp. She's a great kid and a wonderful athlete. Very mature and attractive for her age."

"I guess she played ball for No Hit, said the sheriff. "Did you ever hear the reverend complain about the way he handled her or anything along those lines?"

"No, I got the impression that Deacon wasn't too interested in the ball games. He just sort of went along with it because

Anita was so interested in playing. I hear he hardly ever went to see her play."

"That's what I hear," said the sheriff. "So I don't suppose there is anything to go on there. It's the damdest thing I've ever been into. I can't find anyone who has any idea what kind of a problem existed between the two of them."

"What about Frank McCray? Have you heard anything concerning his whereabouts?"

"Not a word," the sheriff replied. "He seems to have evaporated into thin air."

It was just after noon when the sheriff finished his conversation with Harold Blaney. He didn't have anything pressing him, so he decided he would just go ahead out to the Jorgenson place and see if he could locate Hans. He didn't know much about him except that he ran by far the biggest cow/calf operation in the county. He did most of it by himself with the help of his three sisters. Sidney Curtin had remarked to the sheriff that the Jorgensons had a hell of a bank account and had never asked for a loan.

THE HANS JORGENSON FARM
OCTOBER 2, 2008

Sheriff McKee drove up the long hollow where the Jorgenson homestead was and crossed over the creek to the house. The house was barely visible from the road but as Clayton pulled up into the yard he was impressed with what a well-kept place it was. He knew a lot of farmers who took good care of their livestock and barn but tended to let the house go to hell. That was not the case with the Jorgenson spread. He figured the three girls had something to do with that.

No one answered the door so he walked around back and saw one of the girls digging potatoes in the kitchen garden a few yards from the house. He didn't know one of the Jorgenson girls from the other, so he just walked toward her and said, "Miss Jorgenson."

She jumped a little because she had not heard or seen his approach.

"I'm Sheriff McKee," he began. "You should have had those potatoes out of the ground and in the cellar by now."

"I guess you're right about that," she replied. "I just haven't gotten around to digging them. What can I do for you today, sheriff?"

"I was wondering if your brother is around."

"I think he and Arlene are out around the barn working on a hay baler. I know they tore one up and they still have a little more hay to get in. I'll walk out with you."

"Thanks," Clayton replied. "Which one of the girls are you?"

"I'm Eileen, the youngest," she said, as she brushed her hair out of her eyes.

Clayton McKee looked her over as they walked toward the barn. She was a pleasant looking girl, well constructed, and kind of pretty in a plain way. He could not help but wonder why none of the girls had ever gotten married.

"Hans ain't broke no laws, has he?" Eileen asked as they neared the barn.

"No, nothing like that. I just wanted to talk to him a little about the shooting down at the Go-Mart last summer."

"Wasn't that something?" she exclaimed. "I read all about it in the county paper. Hans didn't seem very interested to tell you the truth."

They spotted Hans in one of the sheds near the barn. He stood up when he saw them approaching and began wiping his greasy hands on a rag.

"Hello, sheriff," he said. "What in the world brings you up our holler?"

"I wanted to talk with you a bit about Frank McCray if I could. I know you served with him on the Economic Development Committee. Did you ever observe any serious conflict among the three gentlemen who were involved in the incident at the Go-Mart?"

"To tell you the truth, sheriff, I've not had any contact with any of them except at the meetings. As you know, I don't get to town much. But, you know, Frank McCray was my favorite guy on the Committee. He was always friendly and made me feel welcome. I liked him and the Extension Agent. Didn't care much for the rest of them. I was about ready to get off the Committee when all of this shit happened. I just don't have much tolerance for meetings. I ain't heard nothing out of Sidney since the shooting, so I guess the Committee has probably played out. Looks like the economy is going to go to hell anyway. I don't pay much attention to the news but looks to me like America is in one big mess."

"I don't know about that," said Clayton. "I just thought maybe you might have overheard something or observed something among the three men involved in the incident that might help me."

"Fraid not," said Hans.

"Thanks for you time," said Clayton. "You folks sure do have a nice spread here. You ought to be proud of it."

"Thanks. It's a hell of a lot of work is what it is," said Hans. "But I reckon we're stuck with it. You know, sheriff, I hear a lot of people complaining about having to work eight hours a day. But there are no eight-hour days on this farm. It's daylight till dark seven days a week. Sometimes during the haying season I don't get in the house till eleven at night. You know another thing that pisses me off is people whining about having to pay a portion of their hospital insurance. Hell, it costs me about $2,000 dollars a month to keep me and the girls insured."

"I'm sure it's a struggle," said the sheriff, "and I admire you folks for what you do."

As the sheriff was driving back to town, he remembered Sidney Curtin telling him how much money the Jorgensons had in the bank. He was not worried about them.

Hans Jorgenson gave the appearance of being an all-work-and-no play farmer. He put in ten-hour days and thought nothing of it. He was blessed with endless energy and was uncommonly strong. He appeared to have no interest in women. No one had ever seen a woman with him when he made his infrequent trips to town. But there actually was a woman in his life.

The widow, Tesla Harper, lived a couple of hollows over on a sixty-acre spread. Her husband had killed himself on his tractor when Hans was still in high school. After his death, his dad often sent him over to her place to help her out. He had always mowed her meadows in return for the hay. She had fed him many times and always provided him with a cool drink of water when he was working around her place. She was fifty years old, but still a vigorous and halfway attractive woman.

About one year after Hans lost his parents, Tesla asked him to stay for supper after he had delivered her a load of firewood. It was in October. It had been a beautiful, cool, blue sky autumn day. After they had eaten, Hans built a fire for her in her woodstove and started to leave. But she told him that she had been feeling kind of lonesome and wondered if he might stay for a while, just to keep her company.

Hans had no previous experience with a woman. Tesla figured as much. She took a very measured approach. She sat down on the couch with him and touched his arm and shoulders a few times as they talked. She could see that he was very uncomfortable.

"Have you ever been with a woman, Hans?" she asked.

He looked at her for at least a full minute before he answered.

"No, to be completely honest, I never have. I've always liked women but I just have never had time to think about it much. I've always liked you," he said.

She moved a little closer to him.

"Do you find me attractive?" she asked.

"I sure do," he replied. "I've always thought you were a handsome woman."

Tesla put her hand behind his neck and kissed him full on the lips. Hans struggled not at all. He just sort of melted back into the couch and enjoyed the moment.

"Come on upstairs with me," she said softly. "This is only the beginning."

After that fateful night, Hans became a regular visitor at the Harper Farm. His oldest sister, Arlene, soon figured out that something was going on because Hans spent more and more time at the Harper place. Some nights he did not come home at all, but he always returned in time to help with the morning chores. Arlene never questioned him.

She was just sort of intrigued that he had developed some kind of a relationship with a woman.

Even though Arlene was not bad to look at, no man had ever given her a second look, probably because the family was viewed as such a strange clan. Her youngest sister had, over the years, had a few male callers, but they usually gave up on her after a few visits. She had become quite reclusive.

During the month of February, about a year-and-a-half into the affair, Hans and Tesla had cooled off a bit. Arlene noticed that he had not left the hollow for a couple of weeks. He just went about his chores and turned into his room early every evening.

On one especially cold evening, Hans heard a gentle knock on his door around midnight. Thinking something was wrong, or someone was sick, he went to the door in his shorts. He saw Arlene standing there with a button-up nightshirt on. The top two buttons were not buttoned. He could see her breasts moving with her breathing.

"I want to talk to you for a moment," she said. "Can I come in?"

Hans, thinking this was really strange, nodded his head and stepped out of her way.

Arlene came and sat down on a straight-back chair that

was the only chair in the room. Hans sat down on the edge of his bed.

"Hans," she began. "I know that you have been, how is it they say it, screwing Tesla Harper. I want to know how it is. Every now and then I get these internal longings. I suppose they are the result of natural sexual desire. I reckon it's a natural thing that people experience, but I have never had the opportunity to do anything about it. I guess I would just like to know what it's like. Would you consider showing me what you and Tesla do when you go over there?"

Hans was stunned, but he did not say anything initially. He just stared at her and was a little surprised at the beauty of her body. She certainly looked a lot better than a naked Tesla Harper. Finally, he managed a reply.

"I don't know, Arlene. I don't know if I can or not. I mean, hell, you're my sister."

He was, however, getting sexually aroused and Arlene was very aware of the bulge in his shorts. She dropped her nightshirt over her shoulders and walked toward him. Hans picked her up and lowered her onto the bed.

He was very surprised with the experience. Arlene was a much better lover than Tesla. Her body was firmer and she was much more responsive. It was an explosive session. Afterwards, Arlene got up, put on her nightshirt and left his room without saying a word. During the weeks and months that followed, she was a frequent late-night visitor.

SKAGWAY, ALASKA
EARLY OCTOBER 2008

Frank McCraw was now settled into the little flat he had managed to rent for a reasonable price after the tourist season ended in September. The manager asked for fifteen hundred a month but Frank had managed to talk him down to twelve hundred.

It was a comfortable little place with a small kitchen, a bath, a rather small sleeping room and a sitting area. The best thing about it was the location. Frank could walk to just about anywhere he needed to go. He figured he didn't even need the truck, but he decided to hold onto it, at least for a while. There was one thing he discovered very quickly. The cost of living in Alaska was much higher than it had been back home. But he figured he would be financially all right until spring. At that point, he would try to hook up with one of the tourist outfits. He speculated that he did not need much of a job, just enough to survive.

Frank was not too worried about finding something to do to make a living because unlike many professional men, he was very capable with his hands. He could perform just about any kind of handyman work and was a first-rate mechanic. His dad had owned and operated a small car dealership in Pennsylvania. Frank had worked with the mechanics around the garage when he was in high school. He knew how to overhaul an engine before he was eighteen. When he decided his '51 Cadillac did not have enough power to suit him, he replaced the original engine with an '88 model General Motors 350 V-8. He did it all by himself and it worked perfectly. The only thing he was worried about as far a making a living was his identity. There was no way to change your name in the modern world. He was very aware that his social security number would catch up with him sooner or later if he got on someone's payroll.

He had fallen into a pattern in Skagway that he sort of enjoyed. It certainly was a more leisurely life than he had been accustomed to. He didn't have to sit through any meetings. Most of all, he was enjoying not having irate parents harping at him all the time about how many girls were getting pregnant at Transparent County High School. He always wondered what the hell he was supposed to do about it. When he left Transparent County, it was embroiled in a controversy about whether or not to close some of the outlying elementary schools. Frank had mixed feelings about closing the schools. Financially, it was the right thing to do. Yet he worried about taking the schools out of the communities. At any rate, it was no longer his problem.

Skagway had a decent library so he would usually walk over to it each morning and read a little. They got the Wall Street Journal a day late. Frank read it every day and tried to figure out what the hell was going on with the economy. Even though there was no way he was ever going to get to enjoy the money he and Gina had invested, he could see it all evaporating. He would follow the library session with a visit to a little coffee shop where he had gotten acquainted with some of the locals. They were all very friendly. Frank never told any of them that he was from West Virginia. He just told them that he had come up from Montana after a very painful divorce. Everyone seemed to accept that.

He had developed an especially good relationship with the lady who ran the place. Her name was Stella Stuckey. She was an attractive lady, probably in her thirties, who had moved to Skagway with her husband ten years ago. She would sometimes sit down with Frank and talk with him for thirty minutes or so. She quizzed him a little about his marriage and divorce but Frank was very evasive. He learned from their conversations that she and her husband had come to Skagway on a cruise ship and she just sort of fell in love with the place. They went back home to California, sold their house, and brought a few of their belongings up the Alaskan Highway. She said they had both worked for one of the tourist places for the first year, then took the plunge and bought the coffee shop.

On several occasions she told Frank she would help him find a job next spring. She said lots of people would be looking for help. Frank had never noticed her husband around the place so he finally asked about him. Stella said they were separated, but her ex was still in town. She said there was another woman involved.

Frank's only problem was the long evenings. He had absolutely no remorse about shooting Deacon Barger. In Frank's mind, Deacon deserved every one of the seven rounds that he had pumped into him. It had been nearly two months since he shot him and it had not yet disturbed his sleep.

Gina, on the other hand, continued to haunt him and keep him awake at night. He kept thinking about how he had left her with that beautiful place to enjoy for the rest of her life while he would have to grub out a living in Alaska. She would find another man. There was no doubt in his mind about that. She was attractive and well heeled. While she might not be able to re-marry, she would find a man. Frank agonized each evening at the thought of some man moving into his house. Then he would think about the Cadillac and the Mercury. He had brought the titles with him so she couldn't sell them. He had also brought all of the keys. But he could hardly stand the thought of never getting to enjoy them again, not to mention the fact that together they were probably worth around sixty thousand dollars. He would often find himself sitting and brooding over the cars. He tried to think of a way that he could sell them, but there was no way.

Frank was not a drinking man. In fact, he didn't think he had even enjoyed a beer since his college days. But he soon discovered that just about everyone in Skagway liked to drink. Stella had invited him to join her and some of her friends at one of the neighborhood bars several times, but he never got around to going. Then one evening after a rather severe brooding spell, he decided to go down and at least check out the scene.

Stella was sitting at a table with four men. She waved at Frank and yelled, "Come on over." Stella introduced him to everyone. Frank sat down among them and they all enjoyed some conversation and a couple of beers. Everyone was nice and made him feel welcome. Frank drank a couple of beers and to his surprise sort of enjoyed them. They went down pretty good. Then he did something that he had not done in many years. He danced.

He had watched Stella dance with a couple of guys in the group. As he watched, he thought it would come back to him, but he couldn't bring himself to ask her. He and Gina had danced some in their youth, but they had given it up long ago. No one in Transparent County danced. Frank hadn't thought about it while he was there, but after mixing with some of the folks in Skagway, he decided the good people of Transparent County didn't know much about having a good time. He recalled Wesley Fremont's remark at one of the Economic Development Meetings about how they all needed to "lighten up." Perhaps old Wesley was right. Finally, Stella looked at him and asked, "Do you dance, Frank?"

"I used to, back in the last century, but it's been a long time."

"Would you like to try?" she said with a very pretty smile.

"I don't know," he replied. "I might make a fool of myself."

"Oh, come on," Stella said. "When the next slow one plays, we'll do it."

When he finally did get out onto the floor, Frank was surprised at how well he did. He was also reminded how good it felt to have a woman in his arms. Stella was a fine dancer and that, of course, made it easier. A couple of the guys in the group were from the upper mid-west and they liked to polka. Frank watched them swing Stella around the dance floor, laughing all the while.

Frank McCray became a regular at the little bar in Skagway. He came to the conclusion that he was going to get through the winter just fine.

THE NO HIT STALNAKER STORY AND THE CONFESSION

During the spring and summer of 2008, No Hit was going through something of a crisis with his little league teams. Transparent County was a couple of decades behind the rest of the nation, but he was getting pressure to let girls play on the same teams as the boys. He did not like the idea, but he came eventually came around.

For the most part it had been a bad scene. Most of the girls were not athletically inclined and were pretty much a disaster no matter where he placed them. If he put them in the infield, they were totally inept. If he put them in the outfield, routine singles often became home runs. But there were exceptions. To his surprise, a few of the girls showed some promise and showed more baseball savvy than some of the boys. One exception in particular was Anita Barger, the eleven-year-old daughter of Deacon Barger. She might have been the best athlete on the 2008 squads. She hardly ever failed to scoop up a grounder in the infield and could shag a fly ball with any outfielder on the team. Anita did not hit with a lot of power but had a knack for hitting the ball right over the second baseman's head. No Hit immediately put her on the team that he was coaching.

He started her at second base. She played the position as well as any of the boys he had ever coached. What amazed him most of all was that she did not show any masculine tendencies. She was a girl, starting to blossom a little, yet she had all kinds of athletic ability. In addition, she had sort of a natural talent for knowing where to throw the ball once she fielded it. No

Hit felt blessed to have her. She solved the problem of having a girl on his team and he could still win games.

He would let the other coaches worry about how they would handle the girls on their teams. He knew they would all be getting pressure from parents to give them playing time.

One evening when Deacon Barger dropped Anita off for practice, he told No Hit he did not know how much longer he could continue to bring her to practice and come to pick her up. He said that he was still trying to do some backhoe work in addition to his duties at the church. "I'm just having an awful time trying to get her here for each practice. My wife spends a lot of her time running my other daughter to her activities. I just might have to pull her off the team."

"Oh, don't do that," said No Hit. "I'm sure we can work something out. If it comes to that, I can bring her home. You guys live on the other side of town from me, but I won't mind bringing her home. Of course, I won't be able to come get her, but I can bring her home."

"Well, if you can do that," said Deacon, "I guess between my wife and me we can get her here most of the time."

So No Hit began to take Anita home each evening. He had to drive through town and go about five more miles, drop her off, then backtrack to his place. It was about a twenty-minute ride to her house and they became fast friends. Anita did not quite know what to make of the coach. No Hit was so different from her father. He was always laughing, teasing and carrying on. Her dad had always been so serious.

One evening on the way home Anita asked No Hit about his hair coming out. "You are getting almost bald," she teased.

No Hit rubbed his head a little, looked into the rearview mirror and smiled. "I guess it is getting a little slick up there. You probably have more hair between your legs than I have on my head."

Anita giggled a little and replied, "No, I don't, but I am starting to get some growing there."

No Hit didn't respond for a minute or so and then he said, "I think your breasts are beginning to swell a little too, aren't they?"

"Yes," she responded. "My mom has started putting bras on me already."

"I can see that you need one," he replied.

When they pulled into the Barger driveway No Hit looked at her. "You probably shouldn't tell your parents what we've been talking about. They may not like it."

"Oh, I wouldn't," Anita replied. "I would never tell either one of them about such things."

No Hit and Anita had similar conversations about every evening as they made the trip home and the coach began to get sexually excited as they talked. One evening, he could stand it no longer. "Has anyone ever talked to you about sex?" he inquired.

"No, not really," she replied, "but I know what it is. Some of the older boys talk about it and have told me how to get on those internet sites. "I have taken a couple of peeks."

"Have you ever thought that you would like to try it?" he asked.

"No, I think it's kind of gross. I am not sure I see the point of it."

"Have you never played with yourself?" he continued.

"A little," she replied. "I sort of liked that."

When he let her out of the car that evening he had a powerful erection. He began to make plans in his mind.

The next evening, he called practice off a little early giving himself an extra thirty minutes to get Anita home. He turned off one of the roads that led up a hollow where no one lived and pulled down into some brush. Anita did not say anything, but she was very scared. No Hit did not want to rush into anything, so he just taught her about oral sex and the pleasures that it provided. He was quite astonished that she enjoyed helping him more than him helping her.

As the summer progressed, they turned up the same hollow several evenings.

AT THE BARGER'S HOME
OCTOBER 10, 2008

On Friday, October 10, 2008, Sheriff Clayton McKee was late getting to the office. Despite his best efforts, his attitude got worse by the day. With just a little over two months to go as sheriff of Transparent County, he was quickly losing his enthusiasm. He was definitely looking forward to getting out. On this particular morning, he and his wife, Maggie, had lingered over coffee. Clayton loved Maggie a lot. His first marriage had been the victim of too much sea duty. He returned to San Diego after a six-month western Pacific cruise and found divorce papers waiting for him. He met Maggie in Bremerton, Washington when he was forty eight-years old, just after he had retired from the Navy and taken a civilian job in the shipyard there. They had enjoyed some really good years together.

Clayton talked her into moving back to his home turf. She was reluctant at first, but after a couple of visits, she fell in love with the hills. They purchased a beautiful hilltop with a gorgeous view and built themselves a small log house with a wrap-around deck. During the fall of the year the deck provided an absolutely inspiring place to have a morning cup of coffee. It was almost 9:00 a.m. when he finally left the house.

When he arrived at the office he found a note on his desk to call Mrs. Barger. He was intrigued by the note, and immediately called her. When she answered, he recognized stress in her voice.

"What can I do for you this morning, Mrs. Barger?"

"Sheriff McKee, I would like to have a very private conversation with you. Would you be willing to do that?"

"I certainly would," he replied. "Do you want to come by the office?"

"No, I would rather you come down to the house. I think I would be more comfortable talking here."

"I'll be right down," said the sheriff.

He did not tell the girls in the office or any of his deputies where he was going. He just told them he would be gone for an hour or two. He pulled up in from of the Barger house in about twenty minutes. She opened the door before he could knock.

"Come in, sheriff, and have a seat."

Clayton found a seat in a recliner. Mrs. Barger sat down across from him on a couch.

"This concerns my husband and my daughter, and before I say a word, I want you to swear to me that you will keep what is said here between you and me."

"Well, if it concerns your husband's attack on No Hit, I'm not sure I can do that. It is a legal matter, you know."

"Yes, I know," she replied. "But I think you will agree that there can be no charges brought against a dead man. That case is closed, is it not?"

"I guess in a manner of speaking it is, but there is still the case against Frank McCray which must in some way be related."

"I cannot help you with the Frank McCray case, but I now know why my husband attacked Mr. Stalnaker."

"But why does this have to be such a big secret?" the sheriff inquired.

"Because it is all connected with my daughter, Anita, and I see no reason why anyone else needs to know about what happened between Anita and Mr. Stalnaker."

Clayton McKee digested her comments and thought for a few minutes before he answered. "OK, Mrs. Barger, if what you are going to tell me would harm your daughter in any way, I promise it will remain with you and me."

Mrs. Barger began with a steady voice. "Day before yesterday, Anita came home from school and went straight to her room. She would not come out and eat her supper. I thought she had been involved in something at school, perhaps with some of her friends, so I didn't say anything to her. As I prepared for bed about 10:00 p.m., I heard her sobbing. I went into her room, held her in my arms, and let her cry for several minutes. She finally cried it all out. Then it all came pouring out of her."

"I know why Daddy killed Mr. Stalnaker," she said. "I have thought from the very first that I would never be able to tell anyone. I thought I could just keep it inside me. But I just can't. Mr. Stalnaker and I were involved in sex acts for several weeks last summer. I don't know how it got started, but it did. I never told anyone and I am sure he didn't either. But, I just know Daddy must have found out someway. He never said anything to me about it, but I know he found out. Did he say anything to you, Mommy?"

"Not a word, Darling. He never mentioned it," I replied.

Anita did not cry any more. She just sat there and looked at me with a blank stare on her face. My first reaction was I could not believe that the child had kept it to herself for that long. I mean, it's been a couple of months. She went back to school after her daddy's funeral and seemed to be all right. The only thing I noticed was she just got a lot quieter. She sometimes never said a word at dinner. But, of course, I took that to be a natural reaction to the loss of her dad. She went to school this morning and appeared to be OK.

"You know I could have kept this to myself, sheriff, but I just thought you ought to know, and it might help in some way with figuring out why Frank McCray shot him.

But, don't you agree that we don't need to drag Anita's name into this?"

"I agree completely, Mrs. Barger. I told you before you started talking that what you said would remain with me. I am as good as my word. I feel so sorry for that child that I could not do anything to harm her. And you know what? Had I been your husband, I might have done the very same thing. But, as of right now, I still don't see the Frank McCray connection. Guess I'll have to think about that some more."

When the sheriff stood up to leave, Mrs. Barger stood up and looked at him so pitifully that his heart ached for her. He thought she looked liked she needed a hug so he gave her a long one before he left.

BACK AT THE COURTHOUSE
OCTOBER 10, 2008

When the sheriff got back to the courthouse, he noticed a very expensive, top-of-the-line Lexus SUV sitting in the parking lot. He noticed cars. It was a part of his job to notice them. He did not recall ever seeing this particular vehicle before. When he walked into the outer office, one of the girls met him and nodded toward his office. The sheriff paused and looked in. John Wesley Fremont was sitting in one of the chairs waiting for him. He looked just as ornery as he did the day he graduated from high school a few years back.

John Wesley Fremont had learned to live pretty high during his Florida days. After he started making good money, he got himself invited to some pretty big-time parties. He got acquainted with some very beautiful women who knew how to enjoy life. He also got introduced to a drug called cocaine. In fact, he attributed some of his success to the great feeling of self-assurance that the drug provided. He was never quite sure if it was the cocaine or the quality of the women, but his sex life had never been better.

After he had moved back to West Virginia and started his own construction company, he began to miss the social life he had enjoyed in Florida. Those stunningly beautiful women just didn't seem to be around the Charleston area. If they were, he couldn't find them. To his surprise; cocaine was fairly hard to come by unless you dealt with some pretty seedy characters. So Wes began flying down to Florida on weekends. He hooked up with his old friends and partied the weekends away. And even though he was starting to make some pretty serious money, the traveling and partying were getting expensive.

During one of his weekend forays, he was telling one of his Florida friends, a guy whose last name he couldn't pronounce but everyone called Hal, about how the travel was getting expensive and about the lack of cocaine in Charleston. His friend's eyes lit up. "Have you ever considered getting a little distribution business going in that area? I mean, I know you make a good living, but if you can get something going up that way, we are talking about real money, suitcases full of money."

Wes just laughed. "You mean become a dealer? Hell, I don't want any part of that action. I could get my ass thrown in the cooler."

"You wouldn't have to really be a dealer. I could take care of that for you. All you would need to do is to become a transporter and set me up with some high-class contacts.

You know, some of the more sophisticated users just don't like to deal with the bad boys who distribute cocaine. I could provide them with a more attractive avenue for acquiring the stuff. You could just poke around and find out who the high-end users are, pass that on to me, and I'll set up the deliveries. You probably know some of them already. I'm telling you, it could turn into more money for you than you ever imagined. Here's how it could work. You provide me with some names of people in the Charleston area who are users, maybe get me some phone numbers. You just fly down on weekends like you have been doing, but be prepared to drive back. I'll provide you a car. We will load the car for you and someone will pick it up. All you need to do is to drive the car to a designated place in Charleston and park it. You won't even see what you are hauling. I'll pay you twenty thousand dollars a trip, cash money."

"What if I would have an accident or something?" Hell, they'd lock me up and throw the goddamned key away."

"It's just like anything thing else," Hal said. "If you are going to make real money, you have to take some risks. It's no different from investing in the stock market. Those guys take risks, too, and some of them end up in jail."

Wes just brushed off the offer at first. He had peddled a little pot in high school and never got caught, but Hal's offer sounded like a pretty risky game. He had read about drug dealers and transporters getting shot when deals went bad. On the other hand, twenty grand was a hell of a lot of tax-free money so it pressed on his mind all evening. With the American economy going south at flank speed, his business could go to hell in a hurry.

When he lay down that evening he began to think seriously about the deal. With just five trips, he could earn a hundred thousand bucks, tax-free. Twelve trips would earn him a quarter of a million. He met with Hal the next morning and told him he was in.

So John Wesley Fremont became a very high-paid mule making the Florida to Charleston run. He did not make it every week, but made at least one trip a month. It was mostly drug money that built the mansion in Transparent County. The big house in Transparent County was nearly paid for when he drove the last nail. He also paid cash for a new Lexus.

Sheriff McKee walked into his office and stuck out his hand. "John Wesley," he said.

"Good to see you. I've been trying to track you down but you are a busy guy."

"Yes, I know," John replied. "I am usually out on one of the jobs all week, and I spend most weekends in Florida. I heard you were looking for me so I decided to drive up."

"Is that your Lexus out in the parking lot?"

"Afraid so. It's a beaut, isn't it?"

"Good looking set of wheels," the sheriff replied. "You must be doing all right."

"I'm getting by," he smiled. "What is it you want to talk to me about, sheriff?"

"Well, I'm still wallowing around in the Frank McCray thing. I'm not getting anywhere with it. I still don't have a motive, and I don't have any earthly idea where Frank might have gone."

"Isn't that the goddamndest thing?" exclaimed Wesley. "I mean I never had old Frank pegged as a shooter. He was always the calm one. All he ever wanted to do was to putter around with those old cars. I always liked old Frank."

"I think just about everybody liked him," said the sheriff. "He and that cute little wife of his. I am just floundering around with the case, Wesley. One thing I have tried to do is to talk to all of the members of the Economic Development Committee. I know you guys spent considerable time together. I guess I just thought one of you might have sensed something among No Hit, Frank, and Barger."

"Well, shit, sheriff. I guess I would be the last to notice something like that. I missed several of the meetings and had very little contact with any of the members outside the meetings. I heard some of the small talk between them before and after the meetings. You know, at the August meeting they all seemed like asshole buddies to me. I didn't observe any conflict among any of them."

"I am probably not much of a judge of character, but if I would have been asked to guess which one of those guys was capable of violence, I would probably have guessed Cecil Blyer.

I didn't know him until I met with the Committee, but he impressed me as a man who would knock your head off if you gave him any shit."

"I think I would agree," the sheriff replied. "But there is no doubt about the actions of either man. Witnesses saw Reverend Barger beat No Hit to death with a baseball bat and immediately thereafter saw Frank McCray shoot the reverend. Not once, but seven times."

Wesley Fremont thought for a moment or two before he responded. "You know I heard Deacon Barger and No Hit discuss baseball a little. I guess the Reverend's daughter, Anita, is quite a baseball player. No Hit was always bragging on her. The preacher, well, he just sort of seemed a little embarrassed about the whole thing. But their conversations always seemed innocent enough to me. And Frank, hell, he was always so business-like and cordial. You know the only time I ever saw Frank upset was one time at a football game someone leaned on a '55 Chevy that he was sporting around. Now old Frank got pissed about that."

Sheriff McKee smiled and shook his head. "Like I said before, there is no doubt that Frank McCray did the shooting. I'd just like to know why. And, I'd like to know where the hell he went to."

"How about his wife?" Wesley asked. "Have you talked with her? Seems to me she would know something if anyone did."

"I have talked to her once, right after the shooting took place. I got the impression that she was as baffled as the rest of us. But, perhaps you're right. I probably should talk with her again."

"Well, as usual, sheriff, I am no help. I wish I could help you but I am as clueless as you appear to be as far as a motive is concerned."

The sheriff stood up and extended his hand. "Wesley, I really appreciate your driving over to see me. I know you have a million things to do."

"Thanks, sheriff. By the way, I heard that old Charlie Seckman is the new Superintendent of Schools. Is that a fact?"

"Guess it is. At least for a while."

"You know, since I'm here, I am going to drive over and talk with him. I gave him a really hard time when I was in high school, but he always tried to look out for me. I think I owe him an apology and a thank you."

"I'll bet he'd appreciate that," the sheriff replied.

After Wesley left his office the sheriff sat down at his desk and picked up his list of the Transparent County Economic Development Committee. He now knew half the riddle. But he still had no clue about why Frank McCray got involved. He put a checkmark beside the names of Harold Blaney, Hans Jorgenson, Wes Fremont, and Cecil Blyer. None of them had helped him a damned bit.

SKAGWAY, ALASKA
OCTOBER 10, 2008

It was a Wednesday evening in Skagway. Frank McCray was hanging out at the bar with Stella and his new group of friends. They were just sitting around talking and sipping a few beers. One member of the group was a local policeman. Frank did not know his full name, but everyone called him Nick. On this particular evening Nick was sitting directly across from Frank. They were talking about the coming winter and how the roads sometimes became impassable, even down in the panhandle. Suddenly, out of the blue, Nick began a line of conversation that made Frank's heart start racing a thousand miles an hour.

"You say you came up from Havre, Montana. Did you grow up around there?" Nick asked.

"No, I actually grew up in Colorado, came up to Montana to take a job. But I got married in Havre and have been there ever since. At least I was there until the big divorce this summer."

"Have you ever spent any time back east?" Nick inquired.

"No, I really haven't," Frank replied. "The ex and I drove over to Washington, D.C. one time for a visit, but that was it for me as far as the east is concerned."

"Did you drive through West Virginia?" Nick continued.

A chill went up Frank's spine when he heard West Virginia.

"Yes, I think we did go through some of it, passed through some town by the name of Wheeling as I recall."

"I've heard West Virginia is beautiful country," said Nick.

"I'd like to see it some time. I knew a guy from West Virginia when I was in the Air Force. He was always going on about how beautiful it was around where he grew up, Pendleton County as I recall. He said he understood why they called the state 'Almost Heaven' in that song."

Frank just smiled. As soon as he finished his beer he told everyone goodnight and headed to his little flat. He lay awake all night wondering about the conversation with Nick. Why would he bring up West Virginia of all places? He figured that most folks up in Alaska did not even know West Virginia existed. He kept telling himself that there must have been some reason. Old Nick must have seen something in the office or on the computer.

The next morning Frank fired up the Silverado and drove it down to one of the service stations. He got the oil changed, checked out his battery cables, and took a close look at all of his hoses. After inspecting his tires, he decided that it wouldn't hurt to put on a new set. Having good tires was always one of his hang-ups.

He stopped by Stella's place around noon and got him a bite to eat. Stella had been good to him. He really liked her and even harbored the thought of getting something romantic going with her. But he had never gotten around to it. When he left, he did not tell her goodbye, but he tried to tell her with his eyes that he would not be seeing her again.

That afternoon, he got his few belongings into the Chevy and prepared to take off. He knocked on his landlord's door as he made his last trip to his truck. He told him he was going to be spending a few days down in Juneau. He headed the Chevy up the Klondike Highway, picked up the Alaskan Highway, and headed south. His body shuddered a little as he thought about the fact that Nick was about to nail him.

Frank retraced his route down through Canada. His border crossing was a little more stressful as he entered the United States. The American agent checked his passport very carefully and wrote down his name and passport number. He was not sure, but he thought an overhead camera might have taken his picture. Yet the agent was cordial and did not challenge him in any way. Frank drove back through Havre, Montana but did not stop. After an uneventful few hours of driving, he found himself in Cheyenne, Wyoming, on October 16. For some reason or another he decided to drop on down into Colorado and look around for a couple of days. He had always wanted to spend some time in the Colorado Rockies but had just never gotten around to it.

He took I-25 down to Denver, then I-70 West across the heart of Colorado. It was a very scenic drive and he took his time. The next day he found himself in Glenwood Springs. He really wasn't sure why he had headed west. He just decided that he did not want to stay in Denver. It was just another big city and Frank had always had an aversion to big cities. He could never understand why anyone would want to live in one when there was so much open country available.

Glenwood Springs was a neat little town with lots of quaint little shops and restaurants. It was the town where Doc Holiday died. He remembered that. But he was beginning to think about his finances. The money was not going to last forever. How would he ever find a job without revealing his identity?

He had not slept soundly since leaving Alaska. Every time he lay down he would start thinking about Gina living all by herself in their big house. He wondered how long it would be before some slick-talking Charleston real estate agent would be sleeping in his bed and driving his Cadillac. At times he almost thought he was still in love with her because he just could not picture another woman in his life. He had always been very devoted to her.

Frank and Gina McCray had enjoyed a good married life. Their careers had caused them to spend a lot of time apart, but they had both kept their nose to the grindstone and had built a prosperous life together. But during the months right after Gina came into her inheritance, Frank thought he noticed a change in her. She had been spending more and more time in Charleston and had been making all kinds of lame excuses for getting home late. She had been showing more and more houses on Saturdays and sometimes did not get home until midnight. Frank generally amused himself by working on his cars during her absence. Yet he was not happy about the fact that she was hardly ever home when he was.

He had mentioned to her a couple of times that she did not really have to continue selling real estate. He reminded her that they were debt free, had made some good investments, and he was earning a very good salary. But Gina had sort of just brushed that idea off. She told him that she really enjoyed the work she was doing and just did not want to become a stay-at-home wife. "I like to get dressed up and mingle with adult people," she said, "and I just don't want to get involved in civic things."

Frank had dropped the conversation, but he still had some lingering doubts about her behavior. Somehow, she just did not seem the same.

The Saturday following that conversation, Gina left the house just after noon. She told Frank she was going to show a house in South Charleston and then another out on Coal River. "If one of those happens to turn into a sale, I might be rather late getting home," she said.

But when Gina got to Charleston she did not go to her office, nor did she go to South Charleston or Coal River. She turned on I-77 South and drove to the upper end of Kanawha City. She turned into the Knight's Inn and cruised the parking lot a couple of times looking for Deacon's car. He always parked right in front of the room that he had rented. She spotted his car, checked her hair in the rear-view mirror, got out and walked up to room 131 and knocked gently on the door. Deacon immediately opened the door and pulled her inside.

Gina never really understood what it was about the preacher that attracted her so. After she began her duties as secretary/treasurer at the Transparent First Baptist Church, they had spent some time together in his office. There was something about him that just set all of her systems on fast time. When he stood behind her and leaned over her shoulder, her hands would tremble. He was just overpowering. Deacon did not make any moves on her for a couple of years, but she knew that he wanted to. What was worse, she knew that she wanted him to.

He never once tried to kiss her or make any groping moves. He never even tried to brush by her breasts or make any of the other awkward moves that lusty men often made. But one night when they were going over some figures in his office, he got up and walked to the other side of the room. "Gina," he said softly, "I want to ask you something. If I am out of line, just say so, and I will drop it. Do you have any feelings for me like I have for you or am I just imagining things?"

Gina waited for a full minute before she turned to face him. "I guess I would have to confess that all of my feelings for you are not platonic. I have been bothered by this situation for many months and have even thought about resigning."

"Don't do that," he said. "The church needs you too badly. I have thought about this long and hard, Gina. I have decided that I am going to ask you to meet me in Charleston somewhere. Perhaps if we meet where we can be alone we can get this out of our systems. Maybe it will not be what we think it will be at all and we can get on with our lives."

"OK," Gina replied. "You tell me when and where."

The following Friday evening, Deacon rented a room (with cash money that he had taken from the church petty cash fund) at the Charleston House Holiday Inn. When Gina stepped into the room they went into the most passionate embrace that either of them had ever experienced. They simply could not stop kissing each other. The sex that followed far exceeded their expectations. Neither of them had ever known what sex really was until their bodies joined on that fateful Friday night.

From that day forward, they had met at least monthly, sometimes more often, somewhere in Charleston. Deacon often chose a different setting, but he was partial to the Ramada Inn in South Charleston. When Deacon told her he had been using church money to pay for the room, Gina had put all of the money back into the church fund. After that, she provided the money for the room.

As Frank lay brooding in his motel room in Glenwood Springs that evening, his mind went back to June when he finally decided to hire a private detective to follow Gina as she made her rounds in Charleston. He got his first report in early July. It was not pretty. The detective had followed her for three Saturdays. She had gone to a different motel each time. He showed Frank pictures of her entering the rooms and leaving them a couple of hours later. But the photo that put him over the edge was the one of Gina and Deacon embracing briefly as she was going out the door. He had pretty much accepted the fact that Gina was having an affair, but he never once dreamed that it was with Reverend Barger.

He thought back over it. He and Gina had sat in the congregation of the Transparent First Baptist Church on all three of the Sundays following her rendezvous with the preacher. They had listened to Reverend Barger lecture the flock about living right and "doing the right thing."

After he got the report from the detective, he did not confront Gina with the facts that he had in his possession. He just went on with his life as if nothing had changed. He figured if she could deceive him for over a year, then he could fake her out for a few weeks. But two things did change. He did not make love to her a single time after he got the report, and he never went back to church. Gina had gone on to church without him, but she thought nothing of it because Frank did not always go anyway. He was not a religious man. He just went because he thought he should and because he thought Gina wanted him to.

He was not quite sure what Gina thought of his brushing off of her sexual advances. Their sexual activity had slowed down to about once a week anyway. Gina most always initiated them, usually in the middle of the week. He just started telling her he didn't think he was up to it. He hoped she was at least a little worried about it and was wondering what was going on. Frank mulled over the situation during the latter part of July. About the first of August, he decided there was only one solution. That Bible-spouting, hypocrite preacher was going to get his comeuppance.

Frank did not sleep a wink in the Glenwood Springs motel. He lay awake all night thinking about what he was going to do with himself. He still had several thousand dollars in his little brief case but he knew the day of reckoning was coming. He did not feel nearly as safe down in the lower 48 as he had in Alaska. Even though things had probably died down some since the shooting, he knew any moment could spell disaster. The way people got around in modern times; it was quite possible that someone who knew him would see him. Frank thought about that all the time.

He was always very careful not to get stopped in any kind of a routine traffic violation. He figured his name and mug shot was probably on every police computer in America. When the morning finally came, he walked down the street and tried to force down some breakfast. It did not go down well at all.

Back in his room, he looked at himself in the full-length mirror. He noticed that his little pot gut was gone. He figured he must have lost ten or twelve pounds since he left Alaska. There were big dark circles under his eyes. He sat down and looked at his Colorado road map. He decided to drive up to Steamboat Springs.

BLACKWATER FALLS STATE PARK
OCTOBER 9, 2008

Harold Blaney checked into the lodge at Blackwater Falls State Park on Thursday morning, October 9, 2008. There was to be a two-day meeting of the West Virginia Agricultural Extension Agents beginning at 1:00 p.m. He arrived a little early and took a little walk down to the Falls after he got checked into his room.

As he approached the little wooden platform that overlooked the Falls, he was not at all surprised to see Ruby Sebolt leaning over the rail enjoying the mist from the crashing water. She really is quite beautiful, he thought as he looked at her. During the previous week, when Harold informed her that he was going to a meeting at Blackwater Falls, she broke into a big smile.

"Isn't that handy," she said. "Ed has a meeting in Chicago all next week. I will be free as a bird. Why don't I just drive up and join you?"

Harold was excited about the possibility of spending a couple of days with her, but he was also a little nervous about it. Most of the other agents were not very clued in about Harold's personal life. He was not sure he wanted any of them to know there was a woman in his life, especially one who was very married.

"You know, Ruby, that might be a little dangerous for me. The other agents are going to be full of questions if they see me with a woman. Just about every one of them knew my wife before we were divorced. We'll have to be very discreet."

"I hadn't thought about that end of it," Ruby replied.

"Why don't you drive up and check in at the Canaan Valley Resort? It's just a few minutes away. I can slip over there when I have some free time."

"OK, that sounds like a reasonable plan. The last thing I want to do is to cause you any problems," she smiled.

Harold and Ruby enjoyed the Falls for a few minutes before he told her to scurry back over to Canaan. Harold was very anxious to meet her that evening because he had a very bold and exciting proposition for her.

That afternoon Harold sat through some very boring meetings. He thought they would never end. If someone had asked him what they talked about during the sessions, he would not have been able to tell them. His mind was definitely elsewhere. He had dinner with some of the agents and hurried over to the Canaan Resort. It was only about a fifteen-minute drive. He knocked on Ruby's door about 8:30 p.m. It was a warm evening so he asked her if she would like to go for a little walk out around the lodge. He found a well-lighted bench down by what was the ice rink during the winter ski season.

"Ruby," he began, "I have a very important proposition for you to think about. I don't know about you, but I hate this slipping around all the time, living in fear that we are going to miscalculate and get caught. People get shot over this kind of stuff, you know. There may be some rumors around about us, but I don't think anyone has any concrete evidence that you and I are involved. I never thought I would say what I am about to say, but I wonder if you might consider asking for a divorce and marrying me? I mean we have been playing this game for nearly three years. I think it's a miracle that we haven't been caught. And, who knows, maybe everyone in Transparent County is wise to us and we just don't know it. Finally, I have come to the conclusion that I really do love you and would like to spend the rest of my life with you."

Ruby looked at him with what might be called a stunned look. "Harold, I don't know what to say. I'll have to think this through. I'm not sure I could go through all of this and face the people in the county. You know I think the world of you, Harold, but you will have to give me some time."

"You take all the time you need," Harold replied. "But there is more. I have been diligently searching for another job since last summer. I am happy to report that I have been successful. I have been offered an Extension Agent's job in Georgia. I have not yet accepted the position. But if you will agree to marry me, I will put my place up for sale and give two weeks notice. I also want you to know that I dearly love my little place up in the hollow, but I am willing to give it up. I guess what I am trying to say is, I love you more."

Ruby responded with a beaming smile and threw her arms around him. "Oh Harold, I want to marry you, I really do. Can you wait until I can get everything worked out with Ed? He is going to be totally shocked. I'm sure he doesn't have a clue about us.

I have no idea what his reaction is going to be. I have often suspected that there is another woman in his life because he does not pay much attention to me."

"As I said before, I'll give you all the time you need. I'll go ahead and put the place up for sale and call the people in Georgia as soon as I get back home. Have you ever lived anywhere besides Transparent County?"

"No, I haven't," Ruby replied. "Ed and I traveled pretty extensively during the early years of our marriage, but I am definitely a Transparent County girl. Living elsewhere would be a big adjustment for me. My heart is racing a hundred miles an hour, Harold. I don't know if I have the courage to face Ed and ask him for a divorce. And where will I go after I confront him? I'm sure he will throw me out of the house. I guess if I have to I can go spend some time with mom and dad. I suppose they'll take me in."

Harold replied, "I'll go down to Georgia as soon as I can and try to find us a place to get settled. I have some money ahead to make the transition and, if I have to, I do have some assets that I can liquidate."

Harold and Ruby stood up and held each other for a very long time before going to her room.

When Harold got back to Transparent County on Friday afternoon, October 10, 2008, he sat down and wrote his letter of resignation to the West Virginia University Extension Service. He also wrote a letter to Sidney Curtin resigning from the Transparent County Economic Development Committee. He was not sure there was such a committee any more, but he felt like he needed to let someone know that he was leaving.

TRANSPARENT COUNTY, WEST VIRGINIA COURTHOUSE OCTOBER 13, 2008

Sheriff McKee was sitting at his desk about 10:00 a.m. enjoying a cup of coffee when he saw two men with slick-looking dark suits enter his outer office. He watched with interest as they showed their credentials to the girls who worked out front. One of the girls directed them back to his office. They came in with grim looks on their faces.

"Sheriff McKee," one of them began as he stuck out his badge. "I am Federal Marshall Kilo Selmon. This is my partner, Lance Kerr. I'm afraid we have some very unpleasant business to conduct here in your county."

"Is that right?" the sheriff replied.

"That's right," replied Kilo Selmon. "We are going to have to make an arrest of one of your very prominent citizens and we would like for you to come along."

"I'd be glad to oblige," Sheriff McKee said as he tried to think who they might be after.

"As you may or may not know," Marshall Selmon continued, "federal auditors conducted an audit of your local bank a few weeks back. They found some very serious discrepancies. The investigation has been ongoing. Several people who work at the bank have been questioned. All have been sworn to secrecy up to this point. The evidence points to the president, Sidney Alvin Curtin. It appears that he may have embezzled nearly a quarter-of-a-million dollars."

"There must be some mistake!" the sheriff exclaimed.

"Sidney is probably the most respected man in this county. He makes an excellent salary, has made some good investments, and is very well off. He would not need to embezzle any money, surely."

"Well, I'm afraid you are wrong, sheriff. We think we have a very strong case built against Mr. Curtin. There is ample evidence to justify his arrest. We would like for you to come along and lend assistance. In fact, we would appreciate it if you would put the cuffs on him."

"You're asking a lot of me, gentlemen," said the baffled sheriff. "Hell's fire, Sidney Curtin and I have been friends for years. We have hunted together, played golf together, helped each other with home repairs, cut firewood together, and fished all night on the riverbank together. I just simply can't believe that Sidney would do such a thing. If you guys have such a strong case, why don't you just go down and arrest him? You sure as hell don't need me."

"We just think it would look better in the community if you would come along," Marshall Kerr interjected. The sheriff stared at the floor for a couple of minutes and did not say anything. Then he reached for his hat and said, "Well, I guess that's what I get paid for. But I want you guys to know that this is about the most unpleasant thing I have ever had to do in the eight years that I have been in this office."

"No one ever said that police work was pleasant," Marshall Kerr responded. "We do things every day that we don't enjoy."

They all walked outside and got into a big Chevy Tahoe and drove to the other side of town where the bank was located. When they got out of the vehicle, Agent Kerr handed the sheriff a pair of handcuffs.

When they walked into the lobby, Sheriff McKee spotted Sidney sitting in his office alone. He ushered the two agents through Sidney's door."

"Good Morning, Sidney, these two gentlemen need to have a word with you."

Kilo Selmon spoke in very matter-of-fact terms. He did not say good morning or even hello. "Mr. Curtin, I am Kilo Selmon, United States Federal Marshall. This is my partner, Lance Kerr. We have a warrant for you arrest."

Sidney did not say a word. He just stood up with a very sick look on his face and looked at the floor. Sheriff McKee was a little amazed that Sidney didn't even look surprised.

"Please put both hands forward," Marshall Kerr said quietly, "and the sheriff will cuff you. We will then proceed to Federal Court in Charleston."

None of the bank employees knew what was going on until they saw the four gentlemen come out into the lobby. When they saw Sidney in cuffs, the place went dead silent. Most of them knew that the bank had been under heavy scrutiny but none of them had a clue that Sidney was going to be arrested. There were also a few bank customers looking on as Sidney was taken by the arm and escorted out the door. Sheriff McKee was instructed to sit up front with Marshall Selmon. Lance Kerr got into the back seat with Sidney. Not a word was spoken as they drove through downtown. Marshall Selmon pulled the big Tahoe over in front of the courthouse.

"Sheriff, you can go back to your office. We really appreciate your attitude and your assistance in this matter."

Sheriff McKee did not respond. He did not say thanks or even goodbye. He just shut the door and walked off.

What else is going to happen before I can get the hell out of this job, he thought to himself.

TAMPA, FLORIDA
OCTOBER 12, 2008

Wes Fremont got up about 8:00 a.m. Sunday morning. He had partied late into the night and was feeling a little weary as he made his way down to the hotel lobby. He picked up a cup of coffee to go, walked out into the parking garage, hit the elevator button, and rode up to the third level. Wes walked down the first row of cars and spotted the gray Toyota Rav sitting exactly where it was supposed to be. He opened the door and found the keys underneath the floor mat. He took the keys and went back to his room to freshen up a bit before taking off. The girl with whom he had spent the night was still asleep. God, she is beautiful, he thought. He did not disturb her.

He went back down to the hotel lobby and enjoyed the breakfast bar before he climbed into the Toyota. The Sunday morning traffic was light, but it took him a while to wind his way out of the city. By 10:00 a.m. he was headed north on I-75. He stayed on I-75 until he got up to Ocala where he picked up Route 301 and rode on north to Baldwin. He had to be very mindful of the speed traps on 301. The last thing he wanted to do was to get stopped for a traffic violation with a load of cocaine in the back. The four Rubbermaid cartons in the cargo area looked innocent enough, but he was not about to take any chances. At Baldwin he picked up I-10 and followed it over to the 295 Beltway around Jacksonville. He drove north, then east on 295 and finally picked up I-95 and headed north. He still drove carefully, making sure he obeyed all of the speed limits.

He did not know how the Toyota got back to Tampa each

time he brought it up, but it always did. He made his first stop soon after he crossed the Georgia line. Before he got out he unlocked the glove compartment and took out the brown envelope. It contained 200 one-hundred dollar bills. He flipped through some of the bills and put the envelope back into the glove compartment. This was his tenth trip, bringing his total to 200,000 tax-free dollars. He filled the Toyota Rav with gas, got a large coffee to go and continued north on I-95 until it intersected with I-26. He followed I-26 to Columbia, South Carolina where picked up I-77 north. He made a rather long stop in Rock Hill, South Carolina. He enjoyed a late evening cheeseburger and fries before continuing north on I-77.

During his last conversation with his friend Hal, Wes had mentioned that he did not see how they could distribute that much cocaine in Charleston. Hal told him that all of it was not staying in Charleston. He said some of it was even making its way to Pittsburgh. Wes did not really give a damn where it was going. He was just curious about how Charleston could possibly consume that much coke in a month or so.

Wes Fremont rolled into Charleston about 1:00 a.m. Monday morning, October 13. He parked the Rav near the State Capitol Building on Lee Street. It was a quiet residential area. He had parked in the same general area each time, always on the street among other cars where it would not look conspicuous. He generally walked eight or ten blocks back toward the downtown area and hailed the first cab he could find to take him up to the airport where he had left his car.

On this particular night it was raining just a bit. He did not have any kind of a raincoat, so he sat in the car for a few minutes, hoping the rain would stop. After about ten minutes the rain had subsided into sprinkles. He got the envelope out of the glove compartment and stepped out into the street. He was getting ready to put the keys under the floor mat when blue lights came on all around him. Before he could take a step, he was surrounded by three Charleston city police cars and one Kanawha County sheriff cruiser. His heart leaped to his throat as he saw a revolver pointed at him and heard the command.

"Turn around and put your hands on top of the car." Wes turned slowly, laid the brown envelope on top of the Rav and did as he was instructed. Almost immediately one of the policemen pulled his hands behind his back and cuffed him. "You are under arrest," the policeman said, "for transporting a controlled substance with the intent to sell.

You have the right to remain silent until you have consulted with an attorney. Give me the keys to your vehicle."

"That's going to be a little tough to do," Wes replied, "Since my hands are bound behind my back. I dropped them on the street when you cuffed me." The policeman picked up the keys and opened up the cargo area. He took out one of the small Rubbermaid containers. Wes was not surprised to see several neatly wrapped packages of cocaine. The policemen all smiled.

"What's in the brown envelope on top of the car?" one of them asked.

"Look for yourself," said Wes. "I don't remember."

"Well, whadda you know?" said the deputy sheriff who had retrieved the envelope.

"It's full of one-hundred-dollar bills. I think we have all of the evidence we need here."

Wes was helped into the back seat of one of the city police cars and immediately transported to the Kanawha County Courthouse. It was about 2:30 a.m. by the time they arrived. He was placed in a holding room until someone arrived to set his bail. That did not happen until about 9:30 a.m. In the meantime, Wes called Robo Weaver, a Charleston attorney with whom he had snorted some coke on several occasions. Mr. Weaver came down to represent him. Bond was set at $100,000, which Wes was able to meet. He had the assets to handle it. He caught a cab up to the airport, picked up his Lexus and drove on home. As soon as he got into the house, he called his friend Hal and gave him the bad news.

"Someone had to tip them off," he told Hal. "They were definitely waiting for me. I cannot imagine who could have squealed on me. I have not told a single soul about the deliveries. It just doesn't make any sense."

"Did they ask you any questions about where you came from?" asked Hal.

"No, not yet, but I am sure that will come sooner or later. But you need not worry about that. I won't tell them anything. I mean I am in a ton of trouble. But I took the risk and I lost, so I'll suck it up and take the consequences. If you need to contact me, you have my business card. Just make sure you call the home number and not the business."

Hal did not answer. He just hung up the phone.

Wes then called his attorney. He and Robo Williams agreed that he was pretty much nailed. But there was some discussion about a possible plea bargain. That afternoon, Wes drove to Putnam County and checked on one of the houses that he had under construction. He picked up some tools and worked the remainder of the afternoon, just to keep his mind occupied. He drove back to Transparent County that evening and spent the night at home. He returned and worked on the house two more days before consulting with his lawyer again. To his surprise, news of his arrest and not yet hit the Charleston papers, so no one in Transparent County knew anything about it.

On Friday morning, October 17, 2008, Wes decided he would go back to Putnam County and work. He figured that he might as well enjoy his freedom while he had it.

He walked out of his Transparent County home about 7:00 a.m. and got into the Lexus. He turned the key to start the engine and the Lexus blew into a thousand pieces. Wesley Fremont never knew what hit him.

There were no houses nearby, but Homer Falls, his nearest neighbor, about a quarter of a mile away, heard the explosion. His initial thought was that one of the natural gas lines had erupted somewhere up the hollow. He decided to go up and investigate before he went to work. As he passed Wes Fremont's house he saw the charred remains of the Lexus sitting in the driveway. As he eased up the driveway he could see what was left of Wes in the front seat which was sitting about ten feet from the main body of the Lexus. Somehow Wes had remained in the seat as it went flying through the air.

Homer did not get out of his car. He looked at his watch and it was about 7:15 a.m.

He figured that the courthouse would not be open so he dialed 911 on his cell phone.

On Saturday morning, October 18, 2008 the following article appeared in the *Charleston Gazette*:

> *On Friday morning, October 17, an explosion rocked one of the dark hollows in nearby Transparent County. Wesley Fremont was killed instantly when his Lexus, evidently wired with a car bomb, exploded in front of his house when he activated the starter.*
>
> *It was learned that Mr. Fremont, the owner of a very successful home-building construction company, had been arrested in the early morning hours on Monday, October 13, on Lee Street in Charleston. The vehicle that he was*

driving was carrying a load of cocaine with a street value of approximately $200,000. Police also confiscated a brown envelope containing $20,000 in cash.

Informed sources at the Kanawha County Court House reported that Mr. Fremont posted the $100,000 bail and was released during the late morning hours on Monday. He was represented by well-known Charleston attorney, Robo Weaver. Mr. Weaver reported that Wes Fremont had worked for his own construction company in Putnam County for the remainder of the week.

This is the third tragic death that has occurred in Transparent County during the past two months. There was a double homicide at the local Go-Mart in that county back in August. We are told by the Transparent County sheriff's office that there does not appear to be a connection between the two incidents. The investigation of both crimes is ongoing.

THE HANS JORGENSON FARM
OCTOBER 16, 2008

It was sixty degrees when Hans came out of the house after breakfast. It was a beautiful October morning, the sort of morning that makes living in West Virginia worthwhile. He walked back into the kitchen where Arlene was clearing away the breakfast dishes.

"I cut that little meadow high on the hill above the Harper place on Monday. There was not much of it, but it looks like this is going to be a great day to get it in the barn.

As soon as the sun dries the dew a little I'm going to pull the square baler up there with the tractor. I should have it baled by around noon. Why don't you bring up a bite to eat after a while and help me pick it up?"

"OK," Arlene replied. "I've got some stuff to do here around the house but I should be able to make it before noon. Do you want coffee to drink, or would you rather have something cold?"

"I think it might warm up pretty good today so why don't you bring up some cold tea. It might taste good by noontime. I'll gas up the four-wheeler for you before I go. I want you to pull that small hay wagon behind you when you come. We can use it to pick up the bales. We'll stack them in that little shed that sits on the north end of the meadow for the time being. They'll stay dry there and I'll haul them on down later this winter. The barn is pretty much full at the moment.

The sun was shining brightly by the time Hans got the tractor up to the high meadow.

The October sky was a deep blue and the temperature was already in the mid-seventies. The sun felt more like August than September. He had pulled both the tether and baler behind the tractor, so as soon as he got there, he set about the task of raking the hay up into windrows. The sun was doing its job and the hay was curing good. He could smell it. Hans had it all baled by noon. He walked around the meadow and counted them. There were only about fifty bales. The little shed would hold those easily, he figured.

Just then he heard the sound of the four-wheeler and saw Arlene coming into the meadow pulling the little wagon behind her. She was not wearing a hat and he could see her hair glistening in the sun. He pointed toward the shed and she drove over to it.

"That sun is pretty hot today," he said. "You probably should have worn a hat of some kind."

"Oh, it shouldn't take us that long to pick it up, so I should be OK. Do you want to go ahead and pick them up before we eat?"

"Yes, let's do," said Hans. Might as well get it done while I have up a head of steam."

They hooked the little wagon up to the tractor. Arlene drove it along very slowly as Hans walked along and threw the bales on. They could get only about twenty bales onto the small wagon so it took them three rounds to get it all in the shed. The shed was open in front, but Hans figured the hay would stay dry enough.

Arlene retrieved a small ice chest that she had tied to the back of the four-wheeler with bungee cords. She had packed some sandwiches, a couple of pieces of cake, and a half-gallon jar of iced tea.

"Let's walk out to the overlook," Hans suggested. "There's

some nice shade there and we can enjoy the view."

"OK," Arlene replied. "I think the shade will feel good after being in that sun for a while."

The overlook was about fifty yards behind the little shed. The meadow ended abruptly there. There was a very steep one-hundred-foot drop down to a small stream that meandered down the hollow. Sitting under a big white oak tree near the edge, Hans and Arlene could see for about a quarter of a mile down the hollow. The bed of the little stream was strewn with rocks, some of them very large. The banks of the creek on both sides were covered with sycamore trees. Sycamore leaves tend to come off early in the fall in West Virginia. The contrast of the stark white bark on their trunks with the patchwork quilt colors of the maples and oaks gave them an almost ghost-like appearance.

After they finished their lunch, they returned to the little shed. They leaned back on the fresh hay bales and enjoyed the October day. The autumn colors were just about at their peak and the surrounding hills were indeed a sight to behold. The sugar maples were brilliant; some of the oaks were a crimson red, and there were several shimmering beech trees around the edge of the meadow. It was indeed an inspiring scene.

Hans began looking at Arlene, watching her breathe, and observing the swells under her shirt. She saw him looking and stood up. She extended her hands and pulled him to his feet. Hans unbuttoned her shirt and pushed up her bra. He fondled her breasts with his hands and in no time at all was devouring them. He removed the remainder of her clothes, picked her up, and laid her on the last row of hay bales. The bales made a near perfect bed but they were a little scratchy. Hans pulled her up, removed his shirt and laid both his and her clothes on the hay.

As they were beginning to get dressed, they heard a female voice say, "Good afternoon."

They both threw a panicked look toward the voice. It was Tesla Harper, the same Tesla Harper who had taught Hans the joy of sex.

"No wonder you have not been coming over," she said as she glared at Hans." You haven't needed to. But I never once dreamed you were screwing your own sister."

Arlene was struggling to get her clothes on. As soon as she had them on far enough to walk, she hurried to the four-wheeler and tore out of the meadow, leaving poor Hans to face Tesla Harper alone.

"I guess you know that what you are doing is not only immoral and unethical," she said. "It is also against the law. I ought to turn you into the authorities. Also, I guess you realize that you are on my property, cutting my hay."

Hans was totally humiliated. He could not find any words to say as he finished getting his pants on. Finally, he managed a sentence.

"I have been cutting your hay for years, Tesla. You know that."

"Do you have it in writing that I gave it to you?"

"Well, no," Hans replied. "But, hell, look how many years I have been cutting it."

"Hans Jorgenson, you are the most disgusting, despicable human being I know. I don't know what I will do yet, but I'm thinking I should tell the sheriff about you and Arlene.

"Now, Tesla, there's no use getting all worked up about this. What Arlene and I are doing is not causing any harm to anyone. Why don't you just let it go?"

"What would happen if you would get her pregnant? Wouldn't that be a fine howdy do?"

"We are being very careful to prevent that," said Hans.

But Tesla Harper was not convinced that she was going to let it go. Hans had just deserted her without a word. She was still not very happy about that. In addition to that, she could not get over how absolutely disgusting the entire situation was.

"I don't know, Hans. I hope you realize how absolutely nauseating this is."

She turned and walked away.

Hans watched her walk across the meadow and into the woods. If she does go out and broadcast this, we could be ruined, he thought. But he had an afterthought that she might cool off once she got home and maybe would let it drop. He decided that he would let her think about it overnight, then maybe go over and talk with her. Then, he had another thought. If she did squawk about it, it would be her word against his. He wasn't so sure anyone would believe her anyway.

He climbed on his tractor and headed for the house. Somehow, he was going to have to get Arlene settled down.

When he got to the house, he learned that Arlene had locked herself in her room and would not come out. She did not come out for supper. Maxine and Eileen had both gone up and knocked on her door but she would not answer. Neither did she come down for breakfast the next morning. Hans knocked on her door and yelled at her but she did not respond. He got really worried about her then, so he forced the door open. He found her sitting in a chair staring out the window. She would not even turn around and acknowledge that he was in the room. Hans went down and told the girls that he thought she just wasn't feeling well. He said that Arlene told him yesterday up in the hayfield that she felt a little lightheaded.

TRANSPARENT COUNTY COURTHOUSE
OFFICE OF THE MAGISTRATE
OCTOBER 20, 2008

About 10:00 a.m. on Monday morning a woman walked into Magistrate Jubal Brady's office. She had a patch over her left eye, a big bruise on her right cheek, and a bandage on the back of her head. Magistrate Brady walked up to his counter and met her stare.

"My name is Fannie Mae Blyer," she said. My husband beat me half to death on Saturday night. I want to file criminal charges against him. I don't know anything about this sort of thing, so you'll have to help me."

"Did you call the police?" the Magistrate asked.

"No, he came home drunk and in a rage over something. He hit me four or five times, I think. I lost count. Finally, he pushed really hard. The last thing I remember is falling backwards. I guess I hit my head on the corner of a cabinet and everything blacked out. When I came around, he was nowhere to be found. My eye was swollen shut and I felt blood on the back of my head. I called my mom and dad. They took me to the emergency room at the Charleston Area Medical Center. They brought me back home yesterday. I slept most of the day. There was still no sign of my husband. I decided this morning that I would file charges. He could have killed me, and I am scared to death that he will come back."

"Are you sure you want to file criminal charges? You can file a domestic violence claim. I can then issue a restraining order which would prevent him from coming back to the house."

"Cecil wouldn't pay any attention to a restraining order. If he wanted to come into the house, he'd come.

"But if he did, we could arrest him," the Magistrate responded.

"But, I might be dead before you arrested him," said Fannie Mae. "I'd like to have him arrested and put away."

"Well, if you file criminal charges, I can issue a warrant for his arrest and bring him in to be arraigned. But he could still post bond and be free to go. Do you really think he is that dangerous? Has he hit you before?

"Yes, he's hit me before. But never anything like this. He has slapped me around a few times but has really never hurt me. He's a very strong man, you know. There is no way I can keep him off me. Look at me! Do you not think he's dangerous?"

"If that's what you want me to do, I'll issue the warrant for his arrest. Do you know where we can find him?"

"My dad drove by the lumber yard this morning and said that his truck was there. I don't know if he's there or not. But it would be a good place to start. He works all the time, you know."

Magistrate Brady processed all the necessary papers, got Fannie Mae's signature, and called the sheriff's office. Sheriff McKee came on the phone. His caller ID told him who it was.

"What's going on this morning, Jubal? Haven't heard from you in a few days."

"I've got a warrant for the arrest of Cecil Blyer. Do you have a deputy available who can go out and bring him in?"

"What the hell for?" asked the sheriff.

"Well, his wife is here, looking like she has been through a meat grinder. She says that he beat the hell out of her Saturday night."

Sheriff McKee paused for a few seconds before he answered. "Well, for Christ's sake, Jubal. I have lately come to the conclusion that Cecil Blyer is a first-class asshole, but I never dreamed he would do anything like that. I swear to God I don't know what the hell this county is coming to. I've been in this office seven-and-one-half years and there's been more shit come down on me during the past two months than all of the rest of the time combined. Is there something in the water, or what?"

"I don't know about that, sheriff. All I know is I have a battered woman here, half scared out of her wits, and she wants her husband arrested."

"Deputies Engle and Myers are sitting here drinking coffee. I'll send them out to look for him. Any idea where they can find him?"

"His wife says his pickup is sitting at his lumber yard, so maybe that's where he is. If he's not there, maybe someone there will know where he is. Tell them to be careful. His wife says he's a handful."

The deputies walked upstairs to the Magistrate's office, picked up the warrant, and drove out to Cecil's place of business. They walked into the front office and saw Cecil sitting at his desk.

Deputy Engle spoke first. "Cecil Blyer, I have a warrant here for your arrest for beating up your wife. Officially, it is called domestic battery. You'll have to ride down with us and appear before the Magistrate."

"Who the hell said I hit my wife?" Cecil roared.

"I guess she did, Cecil. She filed the complaint."

"I didn't hurt her any, just slapped her a couple of times. She had it coming to her anyway. I don't know what all the excitement is about. I don't think I am going any goddamned place."

"We would like to think that you would cooperate and come along peaceably, but if you refuse, we'll have to forcibly put the cuffs on you."

Cecil stared at them for a full minute before he got up. "OK, I'll ride down there with you and talk to the Magistrate. But I'm telling you, this is a crock of shit."

"You need to tell the Magistrate that, Cecil. Not us. We're just doing our job."

When the three men started up the stairs to the Magistrate's Office, Deputy Myers took hold of Cecil's right arm."

"You take your hands off me, mister. I can walk up the steps by myself. I don't need help from you."

Deputy Engle nodded to Deputy Myers and he took his hand away. When they entered the outer office, Magistrate Brady motioned them on into his office.

Jubal Brady was very informal. "Cecil, before I set your bond, is there anything you would like to say on your behalf?"

"There's plenty I would like to say," said Cecil. "In the first place, I don't think it's anybody's business but mine if I want to slap my wife around a little. In the second place, I didn't hurt her any. I don't know what the hell's gotten into her. I'd like to talk with her."

"Well, I think the people in the Emergency Room at the Charleston Area Medical Center would disagree that you didn't hurt her. She has seven stitches in the back of her head and her eye is swollen shut."

"Seven stitches. Well, Jesus Christ. I didn't do that to her. She must have hurt herself some other way. This is ridiculous."

"I guess we'll settle all of that at the hearing. Meantime, I'll set your bond at five thousand dollars. You can either post it or got to jail."

"Go to jail! Well, if this don't beat anything I ever heard

of. I'm not posting any bail, and I am sure to hell not going to jail."

He turned around to leave the office. Deputy Engle grabbed him by the left arm to restrain him. Cecil came around with a right haymaker and knocked the deputy over a chair. Deputy Meyers tried to pin his arms behind him but was unable to do so. He was stronger than a bull ox. By this time, Deputy Engle had recovered and hit Cecil in the back with a stun gun. Cecil went down like a hog that had been shot between the eyes.

The two deputies got his hands behind him and had him cuffed before he recovered."

"That's it," said the magistrate. "Transport him to the regional jail immediately."

THE FRANK MCCRAY PLACE
OCTOBER 21, 2008

Clayton had called Gina McCray at her home on Monday evening and asked if there was a time that he could come and talk with her. She told him that she would be home all day on Tuesday and would be glad to speak with him if he wanted to drop by. Before he drove out to her place, he sat at his desk staring out the window. He had just gotten the report that Wes Fremont had been arrested in Charleston early Monday morning for transporting cocaine. Somehow he was not too surprised. He had watched Wes grow up and remembered that all through his high school days he was just one step ahead of the posse. There had been persistent reports that he was selling drugs at the high school but no one had ever been able to pin it on him.

On the other hand, just about everybody thought that Wesley had gotten his life in order. He certainly had made a big splash during the past couple of years. But events of the past few weeks had convinced the sheriff that anything could happen.

He arrived at the McCray place about 10:00 a.m. It had been the coldest morning of the autumn thus far. Clayton had noticed scattered frost as he drove from his home to the courthouse. When Gina opened the door to let him in, Clayton McKee was a little shocked. He had not seen her for a couple of months and she did not look like the old voluptuous Gina McCray that he knew. She had lost about twenty pounds. Her cheeks were a bit hollow. He could see all kinds of stress in her eyes. The smile was forced.

"Come in, Sheriff McKee, and have a seat. I'll bet you would like to have a cup of coffee. It always tastes good on the first cold morning of the fall."

"You're right about that, Gina. I would love to have a cup, black if you please.

"I just ran a fresh pot through the Bunn," said Gina. "Let's sit at the kitchen table. It's warm and cozy in there this morning. I turned my furnace on for the first time when I got up and built a little fire in the kitchen woodstove. What exactly did you want to talk about, sheriff?"

"First of all, Gina, how are you getting along? You look like you have lost some weight."

"I have indeed," she said. "I'm just not eating like I should. Seems like everything I put in my mouth tastes like sawdust. To tell you the truth, sheriff, I am not really doing very well. I am almost alone in the world. As you know, both of my parents are gone, I don't have any siblings, and no children. I miss Frank so much."

"Has he not made any attempt to contact you, left a message on the phone or anything?"

"Not a word," she said. "I noticed that he didn't even take his cell phone with him. It was lying on the dresser when I got home on that terrible day. For all I know, he could be dead. That's what makes it so difficult, just not knowing. Frank was a good husband. He was always kind, considerate and attentive. And, you know, most folks didn't know it, but he was an excellent cook. He took good care of me."

"I've never met anyone who didn't like Frank," said the sheriff. "Gina, I know I asked you this earlier, but do you not have any inkling about what caused him to go off the deep end and shoot Deacon Barger?"

"I really don't, sheriff. And I don't understand why he has

not tried to contact me."

"Well, if he's alive and hiding somewhere, he's doing a hell of a good job of it. You would think that the computer network that scans this country all the time would have turned up some trace of him, but I have not heard a word."

"What would happen if he ever did turn up?" asked Gina.

"He would definitely be tried for murder. I know it's hard to believe that Frank would do such a thing, but at least three people saw the shooting, one of whom knew him. I guess there is really no way to know for sure what a jury would do, but he would definitely be tried."

"I guess that's the other part of my grief. What would I do if he did come back?"

"Do you have any friends at all to talk with?" asked the sheriff. "This is a hell of thing to have to go through alone."

"I've had some support," she answered. "A couple of the girls that I used to teach with have been by a few times. They have been very helpful. And the guy who owns the real estate firm I work for has been very good to me. He lets me work when I want to, and that's been extremely helpful. I feel much better when I'm working. He and his wife have even had me over for dinner a few times."

Sheriff McKee got up and walked around the table. He took her hand and pulled her up to her feet. He put his arms around her and gave her a brief hug.

"I really appreciate your talking with me," he said. "If you would happen to hear from Frank, let me know. It will be best for everybody. Needless to say, I will do what I can for him if he ever does come to trial. There must have been some reason for his action. If I can find out why he did it, it might help."

"Thanks, sheriff, you are a good and kind man."

As soon as the sheriff left, Gina broke down and cried. She

cried, and cried, and cried until there were no more tears to shed. She knew exactly why Frank shot Deacon Barger.

She just couldn't understand how he had been so cool about it. He never once broached the subject with her. The most surprising thing of all was his behavior on that fateful morning before he left the house. He appeared to be in good humor and showed absolutely no signs of stress.

She had thought about it for weeks, but she still did not see any reason to confess her sins to the sheriff or anyone else. It was always her conclusion that to spill the entire story would just make her life more miserable than it already was. She had decided that she would just wait and see if Frank came back. If he ever did return and was placed on trial, she would make her confession, but not until then. Sheriff McKee would just have to remain in the dark.

She had one more secret thought. She thought that no matter what the outcome, she would never regret her affair with Deacon. Had it not been for him, she would have gone her entire life never knowing what sex was all about. Those one and two hour sessions with Deacon had provided her with ecstasy that she never knew was possible. She still shuddered every time she thought about it.

Gina McCray dried up her tears, straightened up her face and drove to Charleston. It looked like a good day to sell some houses. She was getting a little distressed about her financial situation. The money that she had in mutual funds had lost over half of its value since September. Like most other folks in America, she was concerned about her long- term finances. The unprecedented meltdown on Wall Street was more than she could comprehend, but somehow she doubted if things would ever return to normal.

Fortunately, the housing crisis had not had much impact

on West Virginia. So far, houses were still selling; banks were still lending money. While there had been some layoffs around the state, things did not look all that bleak. She had sold four houses during the month of October. She glanced at the calendar and noticed there were still ten days to go.

As Sheriff Clayton McKee drove back to his office, he said something out loud to himself that he had been thinking for a couple of weeks. Deacon Barger had been screwing Gina McCray just as sure as hell was on fire.

IN THE SHERIFF'S OFFICE
OCTOBER 21, 2009
2:30 P.M.

Sheriff Clayton McKee got back to the office a little before noon. He had stopped by a restaurant on his way back from the McCray place and talked with some of the locals. He had heard that he was being criticized for not making any progress in finding Frank McCray. No one confronted him as he ate his cheeseburger and fries. Everyone seemed friendly enough. Since he was not running for re-election, he was not terribly concerned about public opinion. He did not really know what people expected him to do.

For all practical purposes there was already a new sheriff. Cooter Graham, an ex-game warden, had won the Democratic primary back in May. As was the case in most of West Virginia, there was no Republican opposition. Cooter was just waiting to be crowned. To his credit, he had not interfered in Clayton's business in any way. In fact, Clayton had not even seen him for more than a month. But more and more, Clayton was beginning to think the Frank McCray case was not going to end up being Cooter's problem.

There had been a ray of hope a week or so ago when the authorities finally got around to scanning the Amtrak rosters at Penn Station. A Frank McCray had caught the Lake Shore Limited to Chicago. Chicago's Grand Central Station reported that a Frank McCray had caught the Empire Builder to Seattle, Washington. But from there it had been a dead end. There was no record of his ever arriving or leaving Seattle.

Clayton knew that Frank was sharp enough not to use any

of his credit cards. That's why he took all of that cash out of the bank. And, as Gina had reported, he did not even have a cell phone with him. He was going to be a hard man to find.

As the sheriff was looking through what little information he had in the McCray file, one of the girls in the outer office came in and told him there was a woman insisting on seeing him, but she would not say why.

"Send her in here," said Clayton. "It's hard to tell what might happen next around this damned place." Yet he was still a little stunned by his next visitor.

"My name is Tesla Harper," the woman said.

"I know who you are," the sheriff replied. "What can I do for you?"

"I guess I want to report a crime."

"What sort of crime?" the sheriff asked.

"Do you know the Jorgensons?" she inquired.

"Yes, I know the Jorgensons," Clayton McKee replied. "I assume you are talking about Hans Jorgenson and his sisters."

"That's exactly who I am talking about," she said. "They are the only Jorgensons around here that I know about."

"What about them?"

"Well, I don't know how to say this rather than just blurt it out, but Hans Jorgenson is screwing that oldest girl, the one they call Arlene."

"How the hell do you know that?" the sheriff asked matter-of-factly.

"How do I know? I caught them in the act. That's how I know. Hans has cut my hay for years. A few days ago I heard his tractor in my upper meadow. It was a pretty day so I thought I would just walk up and talk with him. He hadn't been by my place for ages. When I got up there his tractor was sitting in front of an old shed. I walked right up on them in the act.

That's how I know. Now what are you going to do about it?"

"Did anyone else see them?" the sheriff asked.

"Of course not. I was the only one up there."

The sheriff processed all of that in his mind for a bit before he answered. "I'm not exactly sure that they broke any criminal laws," he said. "It is against the law to marry your sister in the state of West Virginia, but I am not quite certain what the law says about the sex act. I'd have to look into it very carefully before I made any arrest.

Actually, you should probably go up and talk to the magistrate. That is where the case would ultimately end up anyway. You realize, of course, that if this should come to any kind of a hearing, it would be just your word against theirs."

"Maybe so," she replied. "But I know what I saw. I have told several people about it already and no one seemed to be surprised."

"Mrs. Harper, you have to be very careful about spreading things around that you can't prove. You are liable to get yourself in trouble. I would recommend that you be very cautious about this."

"That's about what I figured I'd get from you," she replied. "I'd heard that you are a do-nothing sheriff, just biding your time until you can retire. I'll go up and talk to that magistrate. Maybe he'll do something."

"That's exactly what I'd do, Mrs. Harper," said the sheriff.

After she left his office, Clayton McKee just smiled. Actually, he did not doubt her story. The Jorgensons were just strange enough to do that kind of thing. But he decided he was not going to touch that with a ten-foot pole. As far as he was concerned, that little incident came under the heading of what he called "everyday dirt." If she had accused Hans of abusing a child or beating up one of his sisters, he might have gotten excited about it. Besides, there was no way in hell that Tesla Harper could ever prove that. On the other hand, if she had blabbed that story all over the county like she said she had, the damage to Hans was already done. Sheriff McKee knew that people were only too anxious to believe that kind of stuff.

STEAMBOAT SPRINGS, COLORADO
OCTOBER 22, 2008

Frank McCray was a little surprised as he approached Steamboat Springs. It was just sitting there on a flat plain with a big mountain behind it. It certainly did not look like the West Virginia ski resorts at Canaan Valley and at Snowshoe. Somehow, he expected the town to be larger than it was. One of the reasons he had driven up that way from Glenwood Springs was that he thought the ski resorts might be hiring. It might be possible, he thought, to pick up some work at the Steamboat Springs resort without revealing too much about his identity. At least, he might not need to show any credentials. He was sort of thinking about hiring on as kitchen help. He was pretty good at that sort of thing.

He had been keeping a pretty close eye on the news. The national economic situation was getting grimmer by the day. The reports coming out of the Wall Street brokerage houses were unbelievable. Frank knew that much of the money that he and Gina had invested had lost a large slice of its value. Some of the stocks that they owned jointly had crashed. Because of Frank's interest in cars, they had a bunch of General Motors shares. It appeared that both GM and Ford shares were currently pretty much worthless. Gina was definitely not as wealthy as she had been a few months back. But Frank figured that she was still in good shape. The property she was living on was probably worth a quarter-of-a-million dollars, and it was paid for. In addition, Gina had done well in the real estate market. She had been earning several thousand dollars a month in recent years. From what he garnered on the national news, the West Virginia real estate market had not crashed as yet. Most West Virginians were not caught up in the greed syndrome that had infected some parts of the country. Neither had they purchased houses that they could not afford.

Frank checked in to a small motel in Steamboat Springs, paying the bill in cash. A review of his little briefcase told him that he was down to about twelve thousand dollars. He could not believe how fast the money was going.

He still was unable to sleep. He dozed off a little a few times but always awoke with a start, wondering about his future and thinking about Gina. No matter how hard he tried to put her out of his mind, he just couldn't help remembering how beautiful she looked lying in the bed in the mornings as he stumbled around the room getting ready to go to work. And he had so enjoyed watching her eat the breakfast he had fixed for her each morning.

It was still pretty hard for him to believe that she had taken up with Deacon Barger. She always seemed perfectly happy at home. True, their sex life had slowed down a little, but Frank figured everybody's activity slowed down a little after they had been married for several years. On the other hand, he worried that he had been an ineffective lover. He had not had widespread sexual experience before he got married. Maybe he had just failed as a sex partner. He had heard a lot of men say that it was all alike, and that was sort of the way he felt. Yet after having all of his self doubts, he usually came to the same conclusion. He and Gina had just spent too much time apart. He was always busy with the school system, always going back into town for meetings at night. As he thought back over it, he probably spent too much time out in the garage tinkering with his cars. He recalled some evenings when he would be working on one of the cars and time would get away from him.

It would be two or three a.m. before he got to bed. Still, there was no reason for her to take up with a hypocrite preacher. He still had absolutely no remorse about shooting Deacon Barger. Anyone who would stand up in church and lecture his flock about living a good Christian life, then screw one of his parishioners did not deserve to live.

The more he thought about his future the more he concluded that he had none. Even if he managed to escape the long arm of the law, there was no way he could ever get to the retirement money that he had built up over the years. There was no way he could ever sell his valuable antique cars. There was no way he could ever re-enter the profession for which he was trained. Most of all, he figured that sooner or later he would slip up somewhere and get caught.

A few times he thought about giving himself up. If he got himself a good lawyer, a local jury in Transparent County might show some mercy when they learned why he had shot the preacher. But he figured the most he could hope for would be some kind of a light sentence. There was no chance of an acquittal. He pretty much accepted that. So he always came to the same conclusion on those thoughts. He still had no future.

The next morning he walked downtown a few blocks looking for a place to get some breakfast. He saw a small, independent restaurant that looked inviting. As he approached the door he saw a small sign in the window that said "Short Order Cook Wanted, Inquire Within." As he walked inside, he noticed that there were eight or ten tables and a counter with stools. He sat down at the counter and perused the menu. It was pretty standard fare, eggs anyway you wanted them, pancakes, waffles, French toast, home fries and biscuits. Frank figured he could handle all of that including the biscuits. He usually made a pan of biscuits at home every Saturday morning.

His breakfast went down pretty good. As he lingered over coffee, he decided that he would just inquire about the short-order cook job. He asked the waitress who had served him if the manager was there. "That would be her sitting at the end of the counter there, reading the paper," the waitress said with a smile.

Frank looked the woman over for a moment. She was an attractive woman, probably in her forties. He went to the register first and paid his bill, then walked back and approached her. "Are you the manager?" he inquired.

"Manager, owner, and chief cook," she said with a nice smile.

"My name is Frank McCray and I'd like to ask about the short-order cook job."

"OK," she replied. My name is Leanne. Have a seat there and we will talk about it."

Frank sat down on the stool next to her.

"Bring this man a fresh cup of coffee," she yelled at the waitress.

"Mr. McCray, have you had any experience as a short-order cook?"

"No, I must confess that I have never worked in a restaurant," he replied. "But I have always been comfortable in the kitchen. I have cooked a lot for friends. I suppose the grill is my specialty. Also, I used to have a deep fryer in my kitchen and served up a lot of French fries."

"Any experience serving breakfast?"

"Not on a commercial basis, but I feel like I could fix about anything on your menu."

"Where are you from?" Leanne asked, "and what brings you to Steamboat Springs?"

"I'm from up in the northwestern Montana area, and I am not really sure how I ended up here. But I kind of like the looks of the place."

"Well, Mr. McCray, I might just give you a try. I have not had any other applicants and the sign has been up for a week. I'll give you a try. If I don't like what you are doing, I'll let you go with no hard feelings on either side. Would you go along with that?"

"Sure would," said Frank.

"The job pays eight fifty an hour and if you work out, I might bump it up a little. You will work six days a week. I'll fill in the day you are off."

"Sounds good to me. But I do have one more question, and I am a bit embarrassed to ask it."

"Fire away," said Leanne.

"Is there any chance of working for just cash without setting up any kind of an official payroll?"

"Why would you want to do that?" asked Leanne.

"Well, I don't want to burden you with my personal problems, but I have just gone through a very painful divorce up in Montana. To tell you the truth, I really don't want anyone to know where I am right now. My wife was not happy with the settlement. I am afraid she might track me down and want more."

Leanne smiled. "I've never done anything like that before. I sure don't want to get into trouble with the law, but we might try it for a couple of weeks. However, if you work out, and we get into a long-term situation, I'd have to make you legal."

"That would be fine," said Frank. "Maybe in a couple of weeks, things will look different."

"You can start in the morning," said Leana. "Be here at 5:00 a.m. We have some early breakfast folks in this town. I'll be here to help you get started."

"See you then," said Frank as he got up to leave. On his way back to his room, he mulled it all over. Eight fifty an hour. That will work out to about sixteen hundred a month. A couple of months ago I was drawing about eight thousand a month after everything had been deducted.

But he concluded that he would make enough to pay for his room and feed himself. Now he could stay out of his stash and enjoy a little security.

Frank turned in early. He figured he would have to roll out a little after 4:00 a.m.

But he had a terrible night. He didn't sleep more than fifteen minutes all night without waking up. A couple of times he felt almost nauseated. When he finally got out of his bed about 4:15 a.m., he decided he was not going to the restaurant. He began putting his things together and loading them into his truck. At 5:00 a.m. he was headed east on I-70.

IN THE SHERIFF'S OFFICE
OCTOBER 24, 2008

Sheriff McKee had been out of the office most of the day. Court was in session and he had put in a long day in the courtroom. That was one part of his job that he was not going to miss. It was always a tedious day, and to make it worse, he was not able to hear half of what was said. The judge always put his head down when he talked and Clayton rarely heard a word that he uttered.

He breathed a sigh of relief when he got back to his office about 3:30 p.m. He found a note on his desk from NCIC. When he realized that the note was about Frank McCray his hands trembled just a bit. The note said that a Frank McCray with a passport number that matched the passport number that had been issued to Frank McCray from Transparent County, West Virginia, had entered the United States from Canada. Also, the picture taken of him at the border matched the photo of Frank that Sheriff McKee had posted. The message said that Frank had entered the United States just north of Havre, Montana on October 15, 2008. The authorities had no idea where he went from there.

Clayton read the message a couple of times. Well, I'm a son-of-a-bitch, he mused to himself. That damned Frank has been hiding out in Canada. No wonder no one had seen him. But fourteen days had passed since he had come back into the country. It was hard to tell where he had gone after he crossed the border. But maybe, just maybe, he was headed back to West Virginia. Sheriff McKee was excited.

But there was a problem. The border guard was not suspicious and had just conducted a standard-procedure entry. He did not notice what kind of a vehicle Frank was driving. Worse, he did not get a license plate number.

Sheriff McKee did not know a thing about the geography of Montana, so he got on the internet and begin to do a bit of research. He found out where Havre was located and also noticed as he read about the town that the Amtrak Empire Builder always stopped there on its way to Seattle. His eyes lit up a little when he noticed that. It occurred to him that Frank might well have gotten off the train in Havre and gone up into Canada from there. If he did, surmised the sheriff, he must have bought a vehicle in Havre. He looked a little deeper and learned that Havre was the county seat of Hill County. He found the number of the Hill County sheriff's department.

A female voice answered the phone saying, "Hill County sheriff's office. How can I help you today?"

"This is Sheriff Clayton McKee in Transparent County, West Virginia. I was wondering if I might have a word with your sheriff. I'm sorry I was not able to locate his name."

"He just happens to be here," she answered. "Hold on, and I will put him on."

"Sheriff Baxter," a strong male voice stated.

"Sheriff Baxter, this is Clayton McKee, sheriff of Transparent County, West Virginia. I have a rather unusual request and I wonder if you might help me. This is kind of a shot in the dark, but it might really help me."

"I'll do what I can," said the Montana sheriff.

"We have a homicide suspect who fled our county back in August. We think he might have gotten off the train in your town and bought a car. We do know for sure that he has been up in Canada and is now back in the U.S. I wonder if there is some way you can check to see if a man by the name of Frank McCray purchased a car in your town at some point during the last couple of months. He probably paid cash for it. There would surely be a record where he got a license plate somewhere."

"I can probably run that down for you if you will give me a little time," Sheriff Baxter replied. "Give me your number and I'll get back to you."

Clayton McKee hung up the phone and thought to himself, the old sheriff is not as dumb as some people think he is. In about an hour, the Montana sheriff called him back.

"I think I got what you need," he said. A man by the name of Frank McCray purchased a '98 Chevy Silverado on August 16. Here is the most interesting part, though. He had his permanent license plate mailed to a post office box in Skagway, Alaska."

"Well, I'll be a son-of-bitch," said Clayton McKee, "if you will pardon my French."

"That's quite all right, sheriff, I often revert to French around here."

"I've known this man for years, Sheriff Baxter, and I never figured him for a man who would flee to Alaska. Of course, I never figured him for a shooter, either. Hell, he was the Superintendent of Schools in our county."

"Do you know why he killed somebody?" Sheriff Baxter inquired.

"Not for sure, but I have a secret theory. All I know for sure is he pumped seven rounds of .380 slugs into a local preacher. No one seems to have any idea why, but there were witnesses."

"Well, here's the number of the license plate that was mailed to him. He may or may not be running that plate now, but we'll sure keep an eye out for him. That pickup should be pretty easy to spot."

"Thank you so much, Sheriff Baxter. You have been extremely helpful. I'll put a description of the truck and the license number out on NCIC. He could be anywhere by now."

"You're right about that, and you are most welcome. I wish you all the luck in the world with your quest."

Clayton McKee was elated. He at least had something to go on and was no longer floundering around in the dark. The sheriff was not sure why he thought so, but deep in his mind, he just had the feeling that Frank McCray was headed back to Transparent County. His thinking was that Frank had had a few weeks to think it all over and decided his best option was to come home and face the music. On the other hand, it had been a couple of weeks since he came back into the lower 48, and there had been no sign of him yet. Just the same, he put out an alert to the West Virginia State Police to be on the lookout for the Silverado with Montana plates.

ENTERING TRANSPARENT COUNTY
OCTOBER 24, 2008

Frank decided as he left Steamboat Springs that he would stay on the interstates as he headed east. It was his opinion that he would attract less attention on the interstates than anywhere else. Unless there was hot information out on him, it was highly unlikely that he would be stopped unless he happened to get stuck in some sort of routine road check. He stayed within the speed limit and observed all the traffic signals.

He followed I-70 to St. Louis, Missouri. He drove all day on Wednesday the 22nd, stopping only for gas and coffee. He tried to force down a burger about 2:00 p.m., but it did not go well. He gagged on the burger a couple of times and finished his coffee.

From St. Louis, Frank got on I-64 and drove through the wee hours of the morning when the traffic was lighter. He did not stop again until he was just north of Evansville, Indiana. He was having trouble staying awake, so he pulled off at a rest stop. He slid the seat on the Silverado back as far as it would go, leaned against the door on the driver's side, and put his feet up in the seat. Frank did not really go to sleep but he spent a couple of hours in la la land, somewhere between being half asleep and wide-awake. It seemed that every time he was almost asleep, he would awake with a start. It was breaking day when he finally gave up and pulled back onto I-64 East. He stopped and got a sweet roll and a cup of coffee. The sugar in the sweet roll might do him good, he thought, and he definitely needed the caffeine.

As he suspected, the traffic on I-64 was light. The Silverado carried him along at about sixty miles per hour most of the day. He made several stops for coffee and a couple of gas stops. The truck had been wonderful from the day he bought it. He was proud of his choice. But it did not do very well on gasoline. His best estimate was that he was getting about seventeen miles to the gallon. But he noticed that the price of gas was dropping fast. When he left West Virginia back in August, gasoline was over four dollars a gallon. At his last stop in Indiana, he paid two fifty per gallon. He noticed that lots of people at the pumps were talking about the price of gasoline.

Just about the time Sheriff McKee got the report from Sheriff Baxter in Montana, Frank McCray was just east of Lexington, Kentucky, still rolling east on I-64.

He was extremely tired and bleary-eyed. As he leaned forward a bit and looked into his rear-view mirror, he remembered that he had not shaved since he left Steamboat Springs. He looked pretty scruffy. It was about 8:30 p.m. when he saw the sign that said GRAYSON, NEXT THREE EXITS. He had caught himself nodding a bit behind the wheel a time or two during the past thirty minutes, so he concluded that he had better take a break before traveling on. A motel sign to his left caught his attention.

Frank checked in using his own name and paid with cash. The attendant asked him for his driver's license which he readily provided. As he walked toward his truck, he saw a sign on a bank that told him that it was fifty degrees. There was light rain falling. He expected to go out like a light when he got into his room, but it didn't happen. He lay on the bed for a couple of hours but never fell asleep. There were just too many thoughts running through his mind. Just after 11:00 p.m. he climbed back into his truck and drove on into West Virginia.

At about 1:15 a.m. on October 25th, he entered Transparent County in a drizzling rain. As he approached the road that led up the hollow where his house was located, he turned off his headlights and drove the quarter of a mile with the aid of his parking lights. When he pulled into his driveway, he shut the engine down. He hoped Gina had not changed the lock on the front door. He turned the key in the lock very slowly and heard it pop open. There was not a sound in the house as he approached the bedroom except for the gentle whine of the refrigerator. The bedroom door was open. He stood in the doorway for a moment. He could see Gina's hair in the glow of the night light beside the bed. She was lying on her side. He approached the bed very silently, pulled the .380 out of his back pocket and fired four quick rounds into her back, trying to make sure he hit her heart and lungs. She lurched a little and made a whimpering cry.

Frank did not want to watch her die so he scurried back outside. He opened the garage door to where he kept the '51 Cadillac. He slid under the wheel, put the key in the switch and pumped the accelerator a few times to pull up some gasoline. The Caddy fired faithfully as it always had. Frank pulled the big sedan out into the driveway, sat under the wheel for a minute or two and listened to the big V8 purr. Then he pulled the .380 out of his pocket, placed it against his right temple, released the safety and pulled the trigger.

THE GRUESOME DISCOVERY
OCTOBER 27, 2008

The rain had passed through Transparent County during the night and the late October Indian summer weather had returned. Rural mailman, Judd Frye, always enjoyed turning his Subaru up the hollow where the McCray place was located. It was a beautiful hollow, filled with glowing sugar maples. When he delivered Gina's mail on Saturday morning, the 25th, he noticed a black Silverado parked in the driveway. He also noticed that the vintage Cadillac had been pulled out of the garage. But he did not make much of it, just figured some of Gina's relatives had come by and were helping her keep the place up.

But on Monday morning, the 27th, he noticed that the mail he had delivered on Saturday was still in the box. He also noticed that the Silverado had Montana plates.

Judd was pretty famous for minding his own business so he decided not to investigate.

But as he continued his route, he thought maybe he had better report his findings to the sheriff.

After he completed his route, he called the sheriff's office but was informed that the sheriff was at home. The sheriff was outside tending to end-of-the-garden chores when his wife, Maggie, yelled at him. It took him a while to get into the house.

"Sheriff McKee, this is Judd Frye. This may not be anything that you'd be interested in, but I just wanted to report some unusual observations I made up at the Frank McCray place.

On Saturday I noticed a strange pickup in the driveway. I also noticed that his vintage Cadillac was sitting outside. I didn't think anything about it, but this morning I noticed that no one had gotten Saturday's mail out of the box. I pulled up into the driveway, and I noticed that the Chevy Silverado had Montana plates on it. Also, the old Cadillac was sitting outside. It looked like someone was sitting behind the wheel. I figured that I had better mind my own business, so I went back out of the holler and continued by route."

The sheriff paused for a few seconds, containing his excitement, before he answered.

"I appreciate the call, Judd. I'll have one of the deputies drive over there and take a look. It does indeed sound a little strange."

As soon as he hung up the sheriff walked out to his county cruiser and got Deputy Myers on the radio.

"Clarence, this is Clayton. Do you happen to know if Deputy Engle is around this weekend?"

"Yeah, he's home. I talked to him this morning."

"Well, something has come up. I want you to drive over and get him. I'll meet you guys at the Courthouse in about a half-an-hour."

"OK, we'll see you there."

There was no doubt in Clayton McKee's mind that Frank McCray was home. It was hard to tell what his state of mind would be so the sheriff wanted to be cautious. He did not want to bungle this situation.

It was about 1:30 p.m. when he met the two deputies. He briefed them on the situation. They drove over to the mouth of the McCray hollow. It was about a quarter of a mile to the house. They decided to ease on up the road, but to pull off before they got in sight of the house. When they got out of the vehicles the sheriff gave the deputies brief instructions. "You guys cross the creek here on foot and circle around behind the house. Keep out of sight. There is plenty of cover in the woods. I'll drive on up to the house and knock on the door. You guys just make sure nobody sneaks out the back. Now don't anyone get carried away and shoot unless he shoots at you. It's hard to tell what the hell Frank is going to do. Be prepared for anything."

Clayton was as upset as he had ever been since becoming sheriff as he got back in his cruiser and drove on to the house. During his nearly eight years as sheriff, he had never fired his pistol at anyone. What was worse, he wondered if he really could shoot Frank McCray. It wasn't like he was going after a bad guy. Frank was an old friend. He pulled up into the driveway and parked right behind the Silverado. When he got out, he could see someone behind the wheel of the Cadillac. He approached very carefully and found Frank McCray slumped over to the left with his head leaning on the door. There was an abundant amount of blood on the seat. There was little doubt in the sheriff's mind that Frank McCray was very dead. He left the body undisturbed and approached the house. No one answered the doorbell. The sheriff walked around to the back of the house and motioned for the deputies to come on down. The back door was locked so they all three walked back around to the front of the house. The front door was not locked.

The sheriff was not at all surprised when he found Gina in her bedroom in a tangle of blood-soaked sheets. Sheriff McKee looked at the two deputies. "Somehow I knew it was going to end this way. I don't know why I thought that, but I did. And, you know, it might have been the best ending we could have had. Don't ever tell anyone that I said that."

"I guess most folks will figure out what led Frank to shoot

Deacon Barger. I've had it figured out for a few weeks. But I still don't know exactly how the hell that situation developed in front of the Go-Mart, even though I pretty much concluded that the shooting had nothing to do with "Deacon" beating old No Hit to death. But you know what? No one will ever know for sure why Frank shot "Deacon." They might think they know, but no one will ever know for sure. All of the players are dead."

"Well, why did he shoot him, sheriff?" asked Deputy Myers.

"You draw your own conclusion," Clayton answered. "I'll keep mine to myself."

TRANSPARENT COUNTY SHERIFF'S OFFICE TUESDAY, OCTOBER 28, 2008

By Tuesday morning, October 28, 2008 word of the apparent murder/suicide in Transparent County had made it to Charleston. Sheriff McKee's office was under siege by 9:00 a.m. The local television stations all had a van on the scene. Reporters from both Charleston newspapers were in front of the courthouse when the sheriff arrived for work. He had been thinking about the situation on the way to work and decided that the way to handle things was to schedule a press conference for 9:30 a.m. He made that announcement to the waiting news media as he approached the front door of the courthouse. "I'll be conducting a news conference right here in front of the courthouse at 9:30, just as soon as I can get things set up."

But that wasn't good enough for the news hounds. They starting shouting questions at him and trying to stick a microphone in front of his face. He heard two or three people shout the same question: "Is this murder/suicide related to the double homicide that occurred last August?" Clayton ignored the question and went on inside. There were two deputies and four state troopers on hand to keep order. While the reporters waited for the new conference, they walked around the crowd of people that had gathered in front of the courthouse and asked questions of anyone who would talk to them. The burning question was, of course, why did Frank McCray shoot Deacon Barger last summer? They got a multitude of answers as they awaited the news conference.

Sheriff McKee was well prepared when he stepped in

front of the podium that had been prepared for him by the courthouse staff. He cleared his throat and made the following statement with a strong and steady voice.

Just about everything I am going to say here this morning about this tragic event is not supported by concrete evidence. Such evidence might be forthcoming at a later date, but right now all we have is speculation. We can't say anything for sure. It is pretty evident that Frank McCray shot his wife, probably during the very early morning hours Saturday morning, the 25th. He apparently shot himself shortly after that. The bodies were not discovered until Monday morning, the 27th.

We were hot on the trail of Frank McCray last week. We had evidence that he had been hiding out in Alaska and that he had re-entered the lower 48 a couple of weeks ago via Montana. We did not know where he went from there but suspected that he might be headed back home. I thought perhaps that Mr. McCray had decided to give himself up.

When the local mail delivery person informed me on Monday morning that Gina McCray had not gotten her Saturday mail out of the box, and that there was a pickup sitting in the McCray driveway with Montana plates, I knew he had returned.

Unfortunately, by the time my deputies and I arrived on the scene, it was much too late.

I am not going to answer any question about why Frank McCray shot his wife and then himself because I don't know at this point in time. Neither do I know why Frank shot the Reverend Alvin "Deacon" Barger last August. Anything that I would say about either incident would be sheer speculation on my part. I have absolutely no concrete evidence about the motivation for either of those shootings. The investigation will be ongoing, If I do turn up unequivocal evidence, I will pass that on. I would also encourage all of you not to speculate about this crime. Speculation can often lead to the harm of innocent people. I hope you will respect my wishes on that subject.

Ladies and gentlemen that is all I have to say. I will not answer any questions.

Needless to say, the press corps was not happy with Clayton McKee. They all had a list of questions they wanted to ask. They all thought that he should have provided much more information than he did. Some of them even thought he was hiding evidence.

In fact, when the papers came out the following day, there were some questions raised about a possible cover up. One *Gazette* reporter, who had followed the story a little more closely than the others, wanted to raise some questions about the membership of the Transparent County Economic Development Committee. As well as he could determine, three of the members were now dead, one was in jail, and the chairman of the Committee, the former president of the First Citizen's Bank of Transparent, was awaiting trial. All of that would make for a sensational story in his mind. What he did not know was that the other two member of the Committee, who appeared to be innocent, also had problems of their own. One was being accused of incest, and the other was in the process of running off with another man's wife.

The Transparent County murder/suicide was front-page above-the-fold news on Wednesday, October 28, 2008. It had been the lead story on the evening news on October the 27th. But as is usually the case with such situations, things died down quickly. There was still plenty of buzz around town though. Those who gathered at the local restaurants for coffee each morning continued to discuss the intriguing case over and over.

The sheriff was faced with the problem of what to do with the bodies. He knew that Gina McCray did not have any family and that Frank was from Pennsylvania. He had talked with Frank's father shortly after the Go-Mart incident, just to make sure he had not headed home. Just about the time the sheriff started to call the McCray family, Frank's parents walked into his office. Clayton guessed both of them to be at least eighty years old, but they looked to be healthy and alert. Frank's younger brother accompanied them.

After a very sad and uncomfortable conversation, it was decided that Frank and Gina would both be transported back to Frank's hometown for burial. The sheriff was actually very relieved by that decision. That was one less thing he would have to worry about.

THE PRIVATE DETECTIVE'S VISIT
OCTOBER 30, 2008

Sheriff McKee arrived at his office at 7:30 a.m. on Thursday morning, October 30. He could not believe how quickly the furor over the McCray incident had died down. By 10:00 a.m. he had not gotten one phone call or inquiry of any kind about the murder/suicide.

Circuit Court was in session. He sat down to go over the docket trying to determine if his presence would be required at some point during the day. He decided that he might be able to avoid the courtroom today, so he relaxed a little and poured a cup of coffee. Just as he sat back down, one of the girls from out front came in and handed him a business card. "There's a gentleman to see you," she said.

Clayton looked at the card.

SAM SECREST
PRIVATE INVESTIGATOR

"Show him in," said Clayton.

A big, good-looking guy came through the door. He looked to be about six-feet four. There was not an ounce of fat on him. As Clayton looked him over, he decided that he could probably back up the line for any NFL team in the country. He was square jawed, dark, and had a full head of hair. Clayton could see a slight bulge on the left side of his sports coat indicating that he was probably packing heat in a shoulder holster. The man stuck out his hand. "I'm Sam Secrest, private investigator from Charleston. I would like to have a very confidential conversation with you."

"All right," Clayton replied as he got up to close the door. "What do you want to talk about?"

"I read with interest your statement in the Charleston papers about the Frank and Gina McCray murder/suicide. You indicated that you had absolutely no evidence that would provide a motive for either the murder/suicide or the shooting of The Reverend Alvin Barger last August. As you well know, sheriff, a private investigator is sworn to secrecy concerning his clients. I would never divulge information about one of my clients as long as he or she was alive. As a matter of fact, I would not divulge any information publicly even if the client were dead. But as a former big-city police detective, I know how important it is to bring closure in your own mind to a case that has bedeviled you. So I am going to provide you with some information that I know will be helpful."

He laid a manila folder on the desk and started to remove the clip that was holding it together.

"Last summer," he said, "I was retained by Frank McCray to follow his wife when she came into Charleston on Saturdays. Frank provided a description of the car, and he always called me when she left home. I followed her on three separate occasions and took some pictures."

He opened the folder and removed some 8 x 10 glossy, black and white photos. Clayton McKee sifted through the photos. There was one of Gina McCray entering a motel room and one of her coming out of the room. The next one showed a very plain picture of Gina and Deacon Barger in an embrace in the door of the motel, apparently as she was leaving. The photos did not surprise Clayton. They merely confirmed what he had pretty much concluded.

"I shared these photos with Frank McCray some three weeks before he shot the Reverend Barger," said the detective.

"When I showed them to him, Mr. McCray made no comment. He just wrote me a check and said thanks. I had mixed feelings about sharing these with you, sheriff. You can, of course, do what you want with the information. I just have one request and that request is that you do not reveal your source."

The sheriff looked him over for a few seconds before he responded.

"I really appreciate your effort on this," said Clayton. "You can rest assured that I will not reveal your name. As a matter of fact, I am not sure just yet what I will do with the information."

Detective Sam Secrest stuck out his hand, gave Clayton a good firm shake, and turned around and left the office without further comment.

Clayton sat down at his desk and sifted through the photos again. He quickly concluded that he was not about to share the pictures with the press or anyone else.

He walked over to the filing cabinet, pulled out the Frank McCray file and stuck the pictures into the folder.

TRANSPARENT COUNTY COURTHOUSE DECEMBER 31, 2008

The last two months of Sheriff Clayton McKee's term of office as sheriff had been uneventful. To be sure, the Frank McCray case was still the topic of conversations in town. Sheriff McKee avoided as many of those gatherings as possible, especially those morning coffee sessions in the local restaurants. He often told his wife, Maggie, that those morning bull sessions were nothing more than an exchange of ignorance. He much preferred having coffee with her. Clayton was looking forward to more leisurely mornings and not having to worry about his cell phone ringing or the scanner blasting a distress call before he finished his breakfast.

He arrived at the courthouse about 9:30 a.m. for his last day on the job. His staff had planned a little noon luncheon in his honor and the girls were all rushing around making preparations. Clayton had been very popular with his staff. In fact, there had probably never been a better-liked sheriff as far as the staff was concerned. During his eight-year tenure he had often taken them all to lunch and was forever having flowers delivered to the desks of the ladies.

Clayton spent most of the morning greeting well-wishers. The past five months had indeed been a challenging time for him. Sidney Curtin and Frank McCray were among his best friends and he was greatly saddened by their fates. Secretly, he thought that maybe No Hit Stalnaker had gotten what was coming to him. He was not really sure how he felt about the Reverend Barger. But Clayton was convinced that his theory about murder was correct. As he had told Mrs. Barger, anyone is capable of anything given the right motivation. That same thought applied to Frank McCray. Even the most mild-mannered man, if pushed far enough, was capable of murder.

After the goodwill luncheon was over Sheriff McKee went into his office for one final look. He cleaned out the few odds and ends from his desk, thinking he might have needed them one more time. But today was it. He put everything into a small handbag and started out the door. Then he had one more thought. He went to the filing cabinet and pulled out the Frank McCray file. He took out the pictures of Gina McCray and Deacon Barger and put them into his bag. He figured there were some things that people just did not need to know.

He walked down the hall and turned in the keys to his county cruiser, told everyone goodbye, and walked outside where Maggie was waiting for him in their brand new Cadillac Escalade. Clayton had put all the money he had earned as sheriff into a savings account at Sidney Curtin's bank. He paid cash for the Cadillac. He had always wanted one. He figured that General Motors needed the money.

— The End —

ABOUT THE AUTHOR

Mack Samples was born and grew up at Corton, West Virginia, a small community near the Clay/Kanawha County line. He acquired a bachelor's degree from Glenville State College and a Master's degree from Ohio University. He spent his working life as a college professor and administrator and was employed by the University of South Carolina, Glenville State College, and West Virginia University.

In addition to his books Mack has published articles in *Goldenseal Magazine* and *Wild Wonderful West Virginia*. He wrote a weekly column for *The West Virginia Hillbilly* back when that publication enjoyed a large following under the direction of Jim Comstock. He currently writes a monthly column for *Two Lane Livin'*, a successful central West Virginia tabloid published by Lisa Hayes, and Bob Weaver's *Hur Herald*, an on-line publication that comes out of Calhoun County.

Mack is also a well-known musician and square dance caller. In 2003 he was the recipient of the Vandalia Award, West Virginia's high folklife award.

Mack Samples
4331 Obrion Road
Duck, WV 25063
304-286-5006
macksamples@gmail.com

ALSO BY MACK SAMPLES:

- ***DOODLE BUG DOODLE BUG YOUR HOUSE IS ON FIRE***
- ***DUST ON THE FIDDLE***
- ***HIPPIES AND HOLINESS***

(A Trilogy of West Virginia based Novels)

- ***ELK RIVER GHOSTS, TALES, & LORE***
- ***THE DEVIL'S TEA TABLES***

(Collections of tales from the Elk River Valley)

- ***HIGH TIMES IN CORTON***

(A history of the community that was built around the John J. Cornwell Compressor Station, owned and operated by Hope Gas)

- ***SASEBO***

(A cold war novel based in Sasebo, Japan during the 1950s)

CDs BY THE SAMPLES BROTHERS BAND

(Mack, Ted, and Roger Samples, and Buddy Griffin):

- ***SLIGHTLY NORTH OF DIXIE***
- ***ACOUSTIC REFLECTIONS***
- ***BEST OF THE SAMPLES BROTHERS***